S0-BNB-153

Fallen Grace

By Katie Roman

I Nicole, Keep
I love you
on truckin' for ever.

Katie

P.S. You're the queen of the
old west.

Copyright © 2013 *by Katie Roman*

Warning: The unauthorized reproduction or distribution of this copyrighted work is illegal. Criminal copyright infringement, including infringement without monetary gain, is investigated by the FBI and is punishable by up to 5 (five) years in federal prison and a fine of $250,000.

Names, characters and incidents depicted in this book are products of the author's imagination or are used fictitiously. Any resemblance to actual events, locales, organizations, or persons, living or dead, is entirely coincidental and beyond the intent of the author or the publisher.

No part of this book may be reproduced or transmitted in any form or by any means, electronic or mechanical, including photocopying, recording, or by any information storage and retrieval system, without permission in writing from the publisher.

Cover Artist: Skylar Faith
Editor: Stacy Sanford
Printed in the United States of America

To my parents, Mary and Mike, who don't seem to mind I'm a bit strange

One

In the forests of the northern barony of Arganis, a young woman fled for her life. She was a simple farmer's daughter and had nothing, but it did not stop the advancing highway robber. No doubt he, like others of his sort, was moving steadily south toward the capital of Cesernan. They came into the small port the barony supported and moved southward to the capital for better plunder. Other highway robbers had threatened girls of the village before, but young Nina did not think she would ever be among them.

Nina's legs ached from running, but she knew he would soon be on her. She had been warned of the dangers of coming home past dark. Her father insisted she stay at her grandmother's should the sun set before her chores were completed, but she decided to return home in spite of the warnings. As her body labored forward to avoid capture, she knew the folly of her choice.

"Come on, poppet, jus' a lit'le kiss for ol' Robbie!" A large hand grabbed the back of Nina's neck. "Play nice wit' us, love. We won't bite."

"Please, I beg you to let me go! I have nothing!" She struggled to get free, but Robbie would have none of that. He was a bear of a man. Years of living life on the underbelly made his hands callused and rough, while years toiling in ship yards made his arms strong like hunters' traps. Nina tried to pull away, but Robbie had her.

"There's always some lit'le thing a woman can offer," he sneered and began to drag her back down the road. Ahead, a light from the guardhouse of Arganis shone. If she could scream loudly enough, the guards who kept the lord's house would come out to investigate.

She kicked and continued her resistance, but the robber easily overpowered her. "Help! Someone!"

Robbie slapped her hard across the face. "No one's gonna come to ya aid, missy. Just you and Robbie out tonight." He put his huge hand over her mouth, stifling any other screams Nina might have had in her. The light ahead didn't move or multiply into torches. The guards hadn't heard. No one heard.

The leaves overhead rustled and Robbie looked up, but there was nothing to see. In his moment of distraction, the farmer's daughter pulled away; ripping a bit of her dress as she started to run again. Robbie was too fast for her. He pulled her back and threw her to the ground, covering her mouth once more. The air was knocked from her lungs. She tried to cry, but only a whimper emerged.

"Ya really is a stupid girl, ain't ya?"

The trees rustled again, but he did not heed it this time. He figured it was nothing more than a small woodland creature. That would be his downfall. Robbie did not see the figure jump from the low branches of the trees and land soundlessly behind him. The young girl did.

"Ready to meet your makers, little girl?"

"The question is, are you?" an icy voice spoke from behind the highwayman.

Robbie turned and saw a figure outfitted as an executioner. Two pale eyes peered out from under an executioner's hood and gleamed in the moonlight. A sword was drawn and pointed directly at Robbie. The figure was small, short and scrawny, and he didn't look as though he would be able to take down a beast like Robbie.

"What's this? A little boy playing dress-up? Ain't that a game for the girls of your village?" the robber asked with a chuckle. "Run along home, boy. This is a man's job."

Robbie reached out to grab the sword arm of the figure, but he was too slow. The executioner moved faster than Robbie had seen anyone move in a long time. His skill with the sword was far from superb, but there was some amount of training there. Whoever this boy in dress up was, he had been given instruction on sword play from a master. More instruction than the highway robber had with weapons, in any event. In the past, Robbie used brute force rather than skill. It had never been a problem before.

Robbie barely felt a thing. The farmer's daughter screamed in disgust and horror as the scarred hand of the robber opened up; his blood spilling onto the ground. It was dark, but the moon provided enough light for her to see the blood pooling. The executioner moved swiftly and lifted his sword up for another blow.

Robbie pulled back in fear, clutching his wrist, shocked anyone dared to cut him. The figure advanced and Robbie pulled away and fled as the figure prepared for a second assault. Nina looked at the blood now seeping into the ground. She had seen the slaughter of pigs and cattle, but never before had she witnessed the attempted dismemberment of a human. She cringed.

Turning his attention to the girl, the executioner sheathed his sword. "Are you all right?" He held out a hand, but she refused it and got to her feet on her own.

"I'm fine." The executioner nodded and pointed up the road. The scuffle between Robbie and the swordsman garnered the attention of the guards. They must have been roused by the highwayman's agonized screams.

The figure nodded to the guardsmen who ran up the path with their weapons drawn. "Who dares to disturb the peace? We've punishments for men like you!"

"Wait!" Nina put herself between the three guards, two archers and one swordsman. "The real troublemaker fled into the forest. This man saved my life."

"I mean only to help, so please excuse me, gentlemen." The executioner's voice was but a whisper. Taking a few steps off the beaten path, the hooded figure fled into the night. The archers shot a few arrows blindly into the dark.

"Stop!" Nina protested.

"Miss, did any harm come to you?" the swordsman asked; taking Nina by the elbow.

The group of four headed back to the guardhouse. "Suppose we should go after that one?" a tall, ginger-haired archer asked. He motioned his bow to the spot where the executioner disappeared off the road.

"No!" Nina cried; clutching fast to the archer's wrist. "He had a chance to hurt me, but he spared me."

The other archer, a lean, bearded blond said, "He's a hero, then."

"We'll let his Lordship decide what our masked friend is," the swordsman, who was clearly the leader, said. "Right now it is our duty to see this young woman home and return to our posts. Tomorrow his Lordship George can be notified of what we saw."

~*~*~

In the port city of Glenbard, Cesernan's key port, everyone was buzzing with the news of a man who rode through the lands held by and adjacent to the barony Arganis. He helped anyone who called for aid, whether they be rich or poor. It was something virtually unheard of. No one had cared about the lower classes in recent memory, and even the royal guards in the city only protected those who had money to be protected. Sure, a knight seeking attention or a knight with a good heart would occasionally do something to see that those without the funds for bribes were taken care of; however, their good deeds did not last for one reason or another. It was nothing like the activities of the man in Arganis. He persisted, night after night. He had been going about this hero business for nearly six months now, and he showed no signs of stopping.

"It's about time someone gave a damn about us in the muck and filth. The Death Dealer is actually keeping our northern brothers safe, unlike King Frederick's soldiers who claim to protect us," the barkeeper of Angel's Tavern said when the latest bit of news hit the city.

"'The Death Dealer'…such a foul name. Has he even killed anyone yet?" a teenage girl asked.

"Ridley, you foolish thing, who cares what he's called?" the barkeep said. "Just as long as he keeps protecting the less prosperous people of this kingdom."

"What else do you call a man who runs about in an executioner's hood?" a drunk man in the corner said with a bawdy laugh. "I suppose 'The Primrose Protector' is more suited

4

to your female sensitivities?"

"Or mayhap 'The Daisy Defender'!" another drunken fool called out; raising his tankard to the sky. "To our beloved hero, The Daisy Defender!"

Ridley rolled her eyes. "But he could have other, grander names. 'The Death Dealer' is too low brow for such a great hero."

"A great hero?" The tavern fell silent as the brooding figure in the corner spoke. Very few in the tavern had seen him move from his spot, much less speak openly.

"Yes, a great hero, Jack," Ridley snapped. "He cares about us downtrodden folk. And maybe someday he'll make his way here to look after us."

"Cares? He sounds rather like a self-serving hero to me. Rides around Arganis on a fine horse with a fine sword. He's got money backing him, and that's no mistake. I say this Death Dealer should be handing out some of his wealth, rather than trying to look after the poor in the north. That would really help. He's probably some nobleman looking for favor in the court's eyes. Once he gains that, he will forget about us. They always do." Jack was right there. The other nobles who helped only wanted to show the king they weren't just glory hounds. But none before had hidden their identities. They paraded themselves around in front of influential members of Frederick's court.

"You sound awfully sure of yourself, Jack," the barkeep said. "But you can't honestly believe this man will abandon us as other nobles have. I mean, look at-"

"*Look at the lives he's saved*, I know. *Look how he hides his face so he may avoid being discovered*; I know that as well. But mark my words, once he gets what he wants, the Death Dealer will be done with us. Heroes are fleeting men who serve no one but themselves." Jack fell silent and returned to his ale, leaving everyone to ponder his words.

Two

Tristan Mullery of Escion came from the southernmost area of Cesernan. When Tristan was a young boy, his father, the Duke of Escion, sent him to become a knight in the kingdom's main city of Ursana. For years Tristan trained hard and long, until his eighteenth birthday came around and he was knighted by Frederick. He survived the trials, took his oaths, and was now proud to carry the banner of Escion for his king and country.

Tristan returned to Escion to learn how to run the land. For one day, he would take his father's place as the Duke. As tradition dictated, the king could call upon him when war threatened the land or when he was needed for matters of state. Tristan was a fine and well respected knight, and he was being groomed to be one of the finest knights Cesernan had ever seen. He enjoyed most facets of his privileged life…except for the annual tournament. Every year his father made him go into Ursana for the king's tournament.

Tristan tried to avoid going, but there was no way out. He had been going for as long as he could remember, but only in the last two years had he begun to compete. Now that his father was retired, it was up to Tristan to compete in the tournament for the Duke's house in Escion. It wasn't that Tristan disliked the tournament, it was the fact that he never won. The prize of Chief Knight always fell to Sir Benjamin of Salatia. Each year, Tristan left the tournament sullen because he failed to secure a victory; a victory he felt he deserved far more than the poor, country knight. As the son of one of the most prominent noblemen in the country, he shouldn't lose to someone like Sir Benjamin.

Benjamin was a lesser noble from Salatia, and since first becoming a knight, he had dominated the joust. He took first in archery as well, showing that his years of hunting woodland game in Salatia were not wasted. The knight always placed in the top three for the sword as well. It was as though the man was born with weaponry in his hands and victory in his veins. He had become a knight ten years prior, and Tristan believed after he won his shield he'd be able to best Benjamin.

"Beat Benjamin?" his grandfather said with a laugh. "Aye, and mayhap I'll wear a dress and become a midwife!"

Despite the taunting, Tristan still believed he might win. And he was not alone. Many knights fantasized about unhorsing the great Sir Benjamin. Since the joust was the most important piece of the tournament, young, hopeful knights came every year to compete to gain the honor of winning. Yet every year Sir Benjamin won, making everyone else look like a fool. It was as though Benjamin was a born tilter with a lance in his hand. Tristan hated losing, especially to the same man every year. The man was almost thirty, but he was as young and vibrant as if he'd only just won his shield. Twenty year-olds like Tristan and Prince Drake should have been claiming the glory.

And then, of course there was the princess; another great problem plaguing Tristan at the time of the tournament. Princess Elisabeth flirted endlessly with him, and although his parents pushed for him to flirt back, Tristan had no real interest in her. This had not always been the case, however. There was a time when Tristan gladly flirted with Frederick's daughter. She was beautiful and gracious, but she talked too much and that presented a problem. Tristan wanted a woman who was silent, and who listened more to him than he did to her. That certainly was not Cesernan's princess.

Tristan sighed loudly as the caravan from Escion entered the castle gates of the King. All the same houses would be there. The high houses of Actis, Escion, and Ursana would be present. The smaller noble houses and baronies such as Egona, Ghilend, and Rewin would be there. Also, country houses from the smallest fiefdoms would have knights in the tournament. The same faces would all be presented, with the exception of a few knights who had just gained their shields. Tristan moved uneasily in his saddle; annoyed at being forced to be present, only to lose the most important event.

Tristan's mother cast her son an angry glance. "Do not be so moody! And give the Princess some attention this year. I'll not sit

7

in the queen's sewing circle and explain why you dodge her."

"Mother, please. I cannot spend all my time with the Princess. She is nice enough, but she is not quiet for even a moment."

"I do not care. She likes you, and so does King Frederick. Do not hurt your chances of winning his complete favor."

Tristan rolled his eyes and dismounted his horse. He wanted Frederick's favor, but the best way to do that was to win the tournament. If he could best Benjamin, he would have the chance to take up as Frederick's favorite knight; an honor he so richly deserved.

Tristan smiled when he saw Prince Drake coming from the stables. "Drake, you dog." The prince pulled him into a bear hug. "Good to see you," Tristan said; stepping back from the Prince. He looked jovial as always.

"A pity it has to be for the tournament. The same boring tournament where Sir Benjamin always wins. Then my sister always throws herself at him, as do all the young women. And we loser knights are left to wallow in defeat with not even a pretty young girl to comfort us," Drake said; walking Tristan and his horse toward the stables. "This year is going to be different, though."

"Why do you say that?"

"Because *this* year a knight has come from the Barony of Arganis. The hermit Duke sent his nephew."

A silence fell between the two friends. "Arganis?" Arganis's former lord had been a great knight. People at tournaments still spoke of him in reverent tones, and any knights who had lived to see him compete gladly tipped their hats in his honor. Tristan was unaware of any man in the Arganis house who was of an age to win his shield.

"Lord Daniel had two brothers, if you remember. George and Leon," Drake explained. "The older brother George took over the governance of Arganis when Daniel died, but his younger brother Leon has a son who trained and became a fine knight. He just entered knighthood and is ready to compete."

8

Tristan had a few fleeting memories of this boy from Arganis, if Drake was speaking of Calvin Hilren, at least. He remembered him serving as a squire while Tristan was preparing to take his trials and become a knight. They were two, maybe three years apart, but Tristan never mingled with him. He was a squire when Calvin was a page, and it always seemed beneath him to mingle with pages.

"Well then," he said, "why should that change the tournament this year? Newly knighted men compete every year, and it is never of any interest. Don't you remember our first year? Beaten in our first rounds of the joust."

"This knight is said to be of – shall we say – a higher quality than others. Rumors have been buzzing about for days that his father is one of the finest swordsmen in Cesernan, as well as a fine weapons trainer. Certainly that sort of gift passes from father to son."

"Perhaps it *was* worth coming out to the tournament this year. We shall have to see if this Arganis knight can live up to the rumors that surround him." If nothing else, this new knight would provide some new blood to the tournament.

~*~*~

Grace Hilren had only been to Ursana once in her life, at the age of seven; her father's last tournament. That was nearly ten years ago, but things were much as she remembered. She even suspected she was in the same room as before. There were two beds in the room: one great, queen-sized one and a small cot pushed into the corner. As a child, she shared the room with Cassandra. Now at seventeen, she still shared the room with her loyal handmaiden.

The young woman opened the shutters to let the room air out a bit. It was warmer in Ursana, where the king kept his palace, than it was in Arganis. Grace was unused to such sweltering heat this early in spring. At her home it was probably a calm, windy day, perfect for walking about the grounds of Arganis castle.

Arganis was not as rich as some of the other provinces, but it was the most beautiful. Its vast forests and large pine trees were

9

renowned as the best for ship building. Then there was the snow. Snow rarely fell more than to provide a soft blanket on the ground. But when snow did cover the land, the pine trees were at their most beautiful. No other area in Cesernan could boast such beauty.

Right now in her home, the weather was pleasant; certainly not too cold and far from hot. Ursana was different. Spring had only just begun, and Grace already felt as though the blistering heat of summer hit her. This place was loud and too much of a change from the peaceful forests of Arganis.

"A change will do you good," Uncle Leon said. He always insisted he knew what would do her good without asking her first. "You'll see the palace again, and you may be able to take a few days and venture into Glenbard. A young girl like you should be looking to buy pretty dresses, not hiding yourself in the forests."

She sighed. It had been so long since she was away from home. The last time she really ventured anywhere was just before her father's death. Her father had been a lord and a well-respected knight in the halls of King Frederick. Some years past, her father died after being thrown from his horse. His neck was broken from the fall and he died instantly.

As a woman, her mother was deemed unfit to take control of Arganis by Cesernan law, and therefore married her husband's brother and allowed him to govern. Her mother became like a ghost. She barely left her room. She just sat there and lamented for her dear, dead husband.

After her father's death, Grace felt as though her life was a dream. Each day she wandered aimlessly around the castle in Arganis, not speaking or interacting with anyone. Her childhood friends and servants, Cassandra and Donald, were her touch with reality. They feared greatly that she was becoming a ghost like her mother.

It wasn't until Grace turned ten that she awoke from her dream, during a ride through the woods with Donald. He often took Grace out for long rides to see to it that she didn't rot away in the castle amongst the memories of her father. On this particular ride, they came upon a young girl being bullied by some men. Donald scared them off, but Grace sat there, unable to do anything. She hadn't so much as called for help. She realized then that her grief for her father had lasted too long, and she needed to help others whose grief was still near. Grace decided to be selfish no more.

"I shall take up the banner of our guardsmen," she boasted proudly. She strutted about the castle with a wooden sword. "And I'll drive the bandits off."

"Our little Grace is quite a feisty one," servants and guards said. They patted her on the head and sent her to play elsewhere.

Her uncle Leon, the master at arms in Arganis, worked with Grace the same way he worked with the village boys. Leon believed the women of Arganis needed to defend themselves, so he trained some of the village girls as well. While most of the girls were just interested in learning the basics of defending themselves, Grace was interested in weaponry. When all the other girls left, she stayed behind with the village boys to learn sword techniques.

Grace continued by herself to learn the finer techniques with a sword. When she felt she was finally ready, Cassandra helped sew an executioner's hood for her and Grace had a leather jerkin made to fit her small form. It was barely a year ago when she first became what people these days were calling The Death Dealer. She was not fond of the name, but there was little she could do to change that.

She adopted a completely different persona as The Death Dealer. The Death Dealer didn't care for names like Grace Hilren did. Rather, The Death Dealer had one goal: to see to the rescue of those who needed it. Life was different under the hood.

~*~*~

Grace looked out onto the rolling hills of Ursana. She looked past the king's grounds and the town beyond toward the hills. They were a comfort in the hectic world of the court. The chief palace of King Frederick was larger than all of the grounds for the Arganis castle, as well as the town that was placed there. The town that surrounded the palace was a bustling place, even more so with the tournament beginning. The whole experience was overwhelming for Grace. Calvin had insisted that she come with him to the king's tournament. He felt it would do her some good to get away from her mother and mingle outside her usual circle. Grace disagreed. There was little the nobles could offer her. She sighed and looked away from the window. The room was empty, leaving Grace with an uncomfortable feeling. For a palace housing so many noble houses, everything was far too quiet. She should be able to hear others milling about outside her room.

She crossed the room and unlocked one of her trunks. The black jerkin and hood looked back at her. She pulled out the hood and put it over her left hand, her sword hand. "You have already become a legend," she whispered to the hood. The empty eye holes stared back at her. "How does that make you feel?"

A loud rap at the door caused Grace to jump. Footsteps she hadn't even heard approached her quarters. She quickly stashed the hood back into her trunk and slammed the lid shut. "Come in," she called to the knocker.

The plump frame of Cassandra opened the door, much to Grace's relief. Her maid was a young woman of nineteen, with a noticeable fondness for sweets. Still, Cassandra had a soft face with a perfect nose and stunning hazel eyes. Her auburn locks were pulled into a tasteful and practical bun. "Milady, they are calling for everyone to come down to the feast. The King had it specially prepared for the knights on the eve of the tournament. Calvin sent me to find you and yet here you are, unready to go. You're going to be late."

Grace let out a groan she tried hard to suppress. Cassandra looked at her lady and shook her head. She knew Grace Hilren better than anyone, which meant she knew what Grace wanted to do rather than feast at the King's table.

Cassandra softly closed the chamber door and moved closer so Grace would hear her whisper. "There will be plenty of time for that later. Right now you are expected at the feast, and there is no time to change into proper dinner attire. You will just have to go as you are."

Cassandra gave Grace a once-over. The girl had not even bothered to put her hair up. Her dark blonde locks fell past her shoulders, and it looked as though Grace hadn't even taken the time to brush them out since waking up. Her simple dress was forest green with a faded gold trim. The other women of the court would look at young Grace as though she were little more than a servant, but there was no time to change her look. Cassandra blamed herself. If she hadn't been taking in the castle, she would have seen to it that Grace was getting ready for the feast.

"Brush your hair, at least."

Grace scoffed and grabbed her brush off the dresser. A few brush strokes made a world of difference. She looked less like a vagabond now. Cassandra took out a sash made to match Grace's dress. "Put your arms up." Cassandra tied the sash around her lady's waist and arranged it as best she could. "Say it's all the fashion in Arganis. Hurry up – your cousin is waiting for you so he may escort you to dinner."

~*~*~

Calvin looked as though he belonged among the court nobles. His light brown hair was cut short and combed neatly, mirroring the style of most of the other young men at court. He was full of pride for his role as knight and he moved about with ease; making small talk where it was needed. His tunic was a rich blue color, and he displayed the silver hawk of Arganis proudly on his chest as he greeted the other nobles. Grace clung to his arm and allowed him to lead her to dinner. She never thought her cousin was one for such social gatherings, but it appeared now that perhaps he did belong here. On the other hand, she looked nothing like the other ladies. Calvin may have the ability to blend in, but she lacked such a talent. Grace wasn't interested in any of this anyway. She hoped Calvin would allow her to leave as soon as the feast was over.

"Young Calvin of Arganis?" An older woman snaked through the crowd and stopped before Grace and Calvin. Grace immediately disliked her. Her eyes were condescending as she looked at Grace. Her smile was fake and her tone of voice made Grace think one word: patronizing. The servants back home, as well as her Uncle Leon, warned Grace that ladies from high noble houses were different from the country ladies in Arganis. She understood those words a little better after one glance at the woman before her. Her graying brown hair was covered by a sheer white veil. The stunning red gown she wore had an elaborate silver trim that flourished on her dress's skirt; making beautiful, intricate knots. She wore fine silver jewelry and ruby earrings. Grace was duly impressed by the woman's attire, but she quickly gathered that was the most interesting thing the woman had to offer the room.

"Oh, Calvin! It has been some months since you were here last. I believe six months have passed since I was blessed with your presence, yes? When you earned your shield, isn't that correct?" Calvin nodded politely. He had been knighted there in the court of Ursana. Had it really been that long ago? "And I hear you are competing this year. How exciting!" She clapped her hands and politely giggled. Grace forced out a smile when the woman looked at her. She was obviously expecting some sort of response.

"And who is this lovely lady?"

"Duchess Katherine of Actis, may I introduce my cousin, the daughter of Lord Daniel of Arganis, Grace Hilren."

Something flashed in Katherine's eyes as she looked upon Grace again. "Daniel's only child? I am surprised. I thought you would look more like your mother, dear. Lady Dedre was one of the most beautiful women in Cesernan. Yet you are so plain; with your father's eyes, far too wide for a woman, and his small ears. I suppose the small ears become you, though they did no justice to your father's face. And that dress! That hardly indicates you are Dedre's daughter." Katherine smiled again. "At least you inherited your mother's nose; petite and ever so upturned. Perfect. Now, I do hope you will sit near us at the feast, Calvin. I made a special request and would be terribly offended if you took up a seat with the other knights. I must be off now." Grace noted how the invitation was only extended to Calvin.

Grace watched her rush over to a group of other women, ranging in age from girls nearer to her own age of seventeen, to old grandmothers. She hardly believed someone could so casually insult her and then act as though nothing happened. Katherine spoke to the other women and they looked toward her. The younger girls, some already married and pregnant, were giggling, though some tried to hide it, and the grandmothers subtly shook their heads. Dedre's only child had not made the impression the famed beauty would have wanted.

"Do not mind the gossip. The women will accept you soon enough."

Grace looked over at the gaggle of women Katherine was with. The giggles and head shakes continued. The common thought would be that Grace was too rustic, as well as a disappointment and failure in court life. The young woman locked eyes with Katherine and narrowed them ever so slightly. The duchess turned away.

"Somehow, I highly doubt that."

~*~*~

Grace found herself sandwiched between Calvin and the extremely fat Lord of Egona during the feast. Katherine was seated across from her and kept sending disapproving stares her way. The old woman was not impressed with the unsavory look Grace had given her before. It made Grace so nervous and angry, she just picked at her food.

"No wonder you are so skinny," Henry of Egona said; brandishing a chicken leg at Grace the same way someone else might shake a finger. "You are missing out on a fantastic feast. King Frederick really went to great lengths this year. I say that every year, of course." He laughed and patted his belly. "Maybe my tastes are just becoming more and more refined and it becomes possible for me to take note of every spice put into my food. So eat up, girl!"

"I am afraid the atmosphere in this room has caused me to lose my appetite, sir," she said quietly; flashing her eyes quickly

15

in Katherine's direction. The duchess's attention was engaged elsewhere at the moment.

Henry seemed to understand and nodded. "Do not mind Duchess Katherine. She is a hound and you are simply a fresh piece of meat. She will talk about you, and there is little that can change it. All the court women are like that. Even our fair Queen Bethany takes part in the gossiping around here. But you…hopefully you will be different," Henry said; helping himself to Grace's roll. "Most ladies let it go and soon join Katherine's assemblage after taking her verbal abuse in silence. But you are outwardly disapproving, and I do hope you stay that way. It would be nice to have a conversation with a female and not have to worry that what is said will be repeated in some knitting circle."

"So you wish to see me socially ostracized? Disapproving as I may be to gossip circles, I do not wish to spend my adult life on the fringes, always being talked about like a fallen woman." That much was truth. There was simply no mistaking it. Grace had a duty to marry and bear children. From childhood, she always knew that was what was expected of her whether she wanted that life or not. Being a social pariah would not help her achieve her family's goals. She was surprised Henry was so open with her about what he thought of the women and how he hoped Grace would turn out.

"Kamaria, bless you, child!" Grace found it strange Henry called on the moon goddess. Most men invoked Ciro, the sun god, for blessings. "I meant no such thing. I just wish to see one woman who does not repeat everything in that damned circle. Many of the women who veer away from Katherine do not stay long at court. I think the duchess likes to drive them away. For a while Lady Myra," he gestured to a pregnant woman who could be no older than nineteen, "was a pupil of mine. At her father's request, I was to teach her mathematics, geography and history. She, too, was disapproving of the gossip geese, but once she married she apparently forgot. She told me at our last lesson – this being after she announced she was with child – that it would be beneficial to her child to make friends with Katherine. I spoke some words about Katherine, thinking young Myra would never repeat them. Four months ago Katherine was gentle toward me, but now she is ice."

"So I am already socially rejected because I have spoken this long with you?" Confused as she was by his motives, Grace liked this man's honesty and now she only teased him.

Catching on to her game, the older man smiled. "You can never help who you are seated beside. But please try to keep my name out of that circle when Katherine eventually accepts you. And don't look at me with those eyes that say 'she will never have me.' You are Lady Dedre's child, and Katherine was always second to Dedre. She's likely to want to turn you from your mother just out of spite."

"Then Katherine must think all women are as fickle as she. I will keep all you have said in mind, though I think you have little to fear. You are awfully open about your thoughts and feelings of these women. You had no way of knowing my true alliance when I sat down. Perhaps I secretly longed to be in that circle. But sir, you have nothing to worry about, as I said. I plan on returning to Arganis as soon as the tournament has ended."

"I am an old, fat knight who enjoys food over women. I had nothing to lose should you have looked on Katherine as an angel of social integrity," Henry said quietly, and put down his fork for the first time. "The ladies hate me already; a newcomer like you could not have damaged my reputation any more. And on another note, I think you should try to stay a bit longer. The tournament is such a small part of what happens here during the spring and summer months. And if rumors be true, you have not been outside your home since Daniel died. Think about staying for a while. These tournaments are not what they used to be, and new blood is always needed." Grace nodded and Henry smiled. "Every year the same people come out, and it seems so long since fresh faces were seen here. Besides, you bring new conversation and new stories. Calvin has lived in Ursana for so long trying to win his shield that he has no new stories for us."

17

"What about you, Grace?" Grace looked up and found a good number of people were staring at her, expecting some sort of answer. In her conversation with Henry, she missed the larger conversation going on around them. Katherine knew this and a spiteful light danced in her eyes.

"Pardon me?" Grace said. "I did not hear the question."

"We were discussing the vigilante in the north. The one who sees to it that any miscreants traveling his roads find the justice the hooded man thinks they deserve. Our group is split as to his usefulness. After all, his brand of justice conflicts with King Frederick's law and undermines our gracious king's authority. His mere presence suggests he does not believe our king is doing a good enough job protecting his subjects. You are from Arganis; what do *you* think of this Death Dealer who rides around the north and deals with those robbers and such?" Katherine asked. Grace knew she was waiting for her to stumble over her response; to say something unacceptable. And she made her opinion known. Katherine was obviously against the Death Dealer, and she wanted to find another reason to hate Grace.

"It is a vulgar name for someone who has not yet killed, to our knowledge. But I believe he is doing a service by helping rid our fair kingdom of some of those who live only to harm others." Grace paused as all eyes remained fixed on her. "Arganis and her port have long been subjected to thieves, murderers and pirates. It is past time our villagers felt some sort of safety. After all, the guards at the Arganis castle do not have the resources to protect every cabin in the north lands. He may violate King Frederick's rule, but our king has not the resources to protect every person who lives in Cesernan." Grace was an Arganis native, and that alone caused everyone who listened to nod in agreement. Even Katherine seemed to accept this argument.

"I agree," Henry piped up, taking a break from his food. He gave Grace a quick smile before continuing. "This Death Dealer may be going over the king's authority, but he is protecting the common folk, and what is a kingdom without its common folk? Our valiant peasants work the land so we might eat at feasts such as this." He raised his wine glass. "A toast is deserved to those hardworking vassals and to The Death Dealer who is willing to protect them." Others in earshot raised their glasses in agreement with Henry.

Grace looked at Sir Henry and smiled. If nothing else good came out of this trip, at least she found a friend at court.

~*~*~

Out of earshot of Grace's seat, Tristan Mullery wished he was closer to the Duchess Katherine of Actis. Then he would at least have the chance to get a better look at the young woman who came from the Barony of Arganis. If rumors were true, she was Calvin's cousin and the only child of Lord Daniel. This was the first time Tristan had seen her. She spent much of her time locked away in her chambers, and was late coming to join everyone else for the feast. He would have to ask Katherine to introduce them, although from the looks of it, Katherine was not fond of the young woman. Then again, Katherine was never overly fond of young, pretty women who came to court.

Tristan leaned over and whispered to Prince Drake, "The girl from Arganis…is she Lord Daniel's only child?"

Drake nodded. "A reserved thing, isn't she? I have hardly seen her speak to anyone but Calvin and Henry since she came down from her chambers, but there is something about her." Drake paused and looked Grace over. Her face was turned away and she seemed completely immersed in a conversation with Henry.

"I saw her first." Tristan gave Drake a light punch on the arm.

"You did not! I saw her when she first arrived, and I'm your prince. Do you really want to anger your future king over a woman?"

"Perhaps over that woman." Tristan and Drake both looked directly at Grace. As though she sensed eyes upon her, she looked up and met their wandering eyes. A shiver ran down Tristan's spine. A woman had never held his gaze for so long without looking away or blushing. This one just stared back with a great intensity in her gray eyes. It seemed unnatural for a woman to stare so. She was not embarrassed as propriety said she should be.

~*~*~

It bothered Grace to have people stare at her, so in order to deter the stares of people, she was prone to locking gazes until her adversaries looked away. This usually caused discomfort, because no one expected a lady to go without blushing or giggling. Currently the Prince and another knight were looking upon her quite intently. Grace kept her gray eyes fixed on them and stared them down. It worked. The Prince and the other young man both looked away from her piercing stare. Had their code of chivalry and manners failed to list 'staring' on its pages? She sighed and turned her attention to Henry once more.

"Trying to scare off the lads, are you?" Henry was finishing up the last of his dessert, and as he spoke, a bit of pie dribbled down his chin and into his beard. He laughed a bit and wiped it off.

"Trying to stop their staring."

"Let sleeping dogs lie, I always say. If they want to stare, let them. Might show Katherine a thing or two if Tristan of Escion and His Highness Prince Drake are after you. For one thing, she might not think you are plain anymore."

Grace nodded. She was far from plain, but no one here really knew that. As far as anyone was concerned she was only the late Lord Daniel and Lady Dedre's reserved daughter, who did not share her mother's enchanting looks and had her father's piercing eyes. The less everyone knew, the better.

The guests began to follow the King and Queen into the great hall for some after dinner dancing. Grace pushed herself away from the table and curtsied to Henry. It seemed only appropriate, since he was the only one who seemed to see her as a friend and not a plague.

"It was a pleasure to speak to you this evening and hopefully I will have the opportunity again, but for now I am exhausted and am going to retire to my room."

Henry rose from his seat and took Grace's hand; lightly

kissing it. "Do not fret about the ladies of this court, young one. It will improve for you, I promise. Show them what a fine lady you are! Join me in a few dances and then you may head to bed."

"I do not know—"

"It will only be worse for you if you decide not to come to the ball. The rumors will spread quickly that you are a northern barbarian who cannot dance. Your cousin's good reputation won't even be able to save you."

Henry held out his arm. Grace made a face and crinkled her nose, but in the end she took the offered arm. Henry led Grace into the great hall where couples had already begun to pair off. Even Calvin found a young noblewoman to dance with. Henry faced Grace and took her hands gently.

"You are not actually a northern barbarian, are you? You *do* know the dances, I assume?"

"Of course." Grace had been raised like any proper noble girl. She knew the manners for court: how to curtsy, the many different dances, and how to conduct herself in the presence of young men. The only thing her training had not prepared her for was how to handle gossip circles.

The first dance was a quick one. Henry smiled down at Grace and gave her hand a squeeze. "So the rumors that those in Arganis are less than civilized are untrue. You dance as well as any woman here. Perhaps better."

"Your compliments are unnecessary, Henry. I learned how to conduct myself in court a long time ago, just like all the other women here."

"Must be the breeding you have from your mother. She was the most fashionable woman at court before her marriage and your birth. And even after, up until your father's death, she was a paragon of courtly charm." He winked down at her.

The next dance kicked into motion. Henry was ready to lead Grace once more, but Prince Drake cut in. "My Lord Henry, might I have the honor of leading this young lady in a dance?"

"I could not possibly refuse my prince." Henry placed Grace's hand in Drake's and strode from the floor to join the crowd of onlookers. Grace felt abandoned. Henry left her in the care of the Prince! There was little he could have done that would have been worse for her.

Grace panicked inwardly, though outwardly she kept her demeanor cool. The Prince was dancing with her, and that meant that all those not dancing would be watching with a critical eye. She knew for a fact Katherine was not dancing, and she would be watching closest of all.

"There is no need to be nervous, milady," Drake said; smiling down at Grace.

"Who said I was nervous?"

"Your sweaty palms speak for themselves. But worry not; those in court will not speak in their circles if you falter. Not when the Prince is involved, at least. They'll do it behind closed doors so as not to impart my wrath upon them." He was lying, but she liked him for that. Drake smiled and led Grace around the dance floor. They would talk twice as much, closed doors or no, but she appreciated his effort to ease her nerves.

Grace pushed the fear of faltering from her mind. She concentrated solely on the dance steps, because no amount of good graces would save her from gossip, especially if she fell or stepped on Drake's toes.

Drake led her around the ballroom through another song. This one slowed and the Prince slowed with it. Grace felt strange having his hand rest on her waist, and if she continued to dance after this, she knew full well she would falter. After the second dance, Grace decided it was time to turn in for the night. The house banners, the many colored dresses, the talking, the laughing, the closeness to the Prince – it was all too much for Grace to take in. She thanked Drake for the dance and turned to excuse herself from the festivities.

Her exit was apparently not something some of the other knights wished to see. Upon seeing her break from their prince, three swarmed around her. One was the young knight who had been seated next to the Prince; the one who watched her so intently. Looking at him more closely, Grace felt her face getting red. He was the most handsome and dashing man she had ever laid eyes on. The men of the Hilren line were notorious for being short, stocky folk. Calvin had the misfortune of being only an inch taller than Grace and several inches shorter than most men his age. The same was true of her uncles. But this man was tall and muscular, with wavy brown hair tied back from his face. He was beardless and had brown eyes reminiscent of a big, playful dog Grace played with in Arganis. His nose was small and perfect; clearly his hadn't been broken like her cousin's had. He looked to be in his early twenties.

The other two knights were not nearly as handsome as this one. They bore scars and the signs of broken noses. The oldest-looking one was probably closer to his early or mid-thirties, with auburn hair and pale skin. The other was closer to the first knight's age, with dark skin and thick, black hair cropped short. His face was marked by pink and white scars, but his black eyes were happy.

"My lady," the handsome knight who had sat with Drake said. "You don't mean to leave us, do you? Not when so many knights wish to lead you in a dance. Please, favor us with your name, lady."

Grace assumed, and correctly so, that these three already knew her name from the rumors she knew were flying around the room. Still, it would be bad form on her part not to honor their request. "I am Grace Hilren from the Barony Arganis to the north. And who are the fine knights who stand before me?"

"I am Sir Tristan of Escion," the first one said. "This," he signaled to the oldest of the three, "is Sir Benjamin of Salatia, and this rough-looking man is Sir Edmund of the fief Pirate's Bay."

"That pendant you wear..." Grace cast her eyes to the opal pendant engulfed by silver flames that Edmund wore about his neck. "Are you by chance from the spice islands, originally? I have heard the opal was a cherished stone among the Nareroc natives."

Edmund was the first to take Grace's hand and kiss it. He seemed pleased she could accurately place the stone he wore.

"Before conquerors from the northern countries set foot on Cesernan, it was covered in dark-skinned folk like myself." His eyes were filled with mirth. "That was centuries ago, and my father is just as fair-skinned as everyone else, but my mother is from the Nareroc Islands, as you guessed. And the opal is of course the most prized jewel there. It is supposed to bring good fortune. Unfortunately, all the mines that once operated have been tapped of their opal resources." The spice islands off the southeastern coast of Cesernan were famous for their warm jungle climates, spices, crystal clear waters, and dark-skinned natives. Grace was familiar with the histories, but had never met a Nareroc descendant. Most were under the impression that Arganis was a frosty wasteland, and they decided to stay in warmer areas.

She wanted to hear more, but knew it was rude not to acknowledge the others. "And Sir Benjamin of Salatia?" When she offered her hand to him, he took it gladly and kissed it. "I have heard of you. The man who tilts as though he was born upon a horse with a lance in hand. Your exploits with the sword are also legendary, if I remember correctly."

"Aye, that be true." Benjamin talked with a country twang Grace heard some of the peasants around Arganis use. He was not so wealthy a knight as Edmund or Tristan, it appeared. It was possible he was from a house that worked itself up from yeoman and into a king's favor. Finally, she turned and offered her hand to Tristan. "And Sir Tristan of Escion." She recalled some scandal from Escion. It happened just before the final tournament her father competed in, but she could not bring forth any memories about it. All she remembered were hushed tones between her father and her uncles. Her brow creased as she tried to remember what happened, but all she could recall was some form of family disgrace.

Tristan misread her expression and stated, "I realize I am not as renowned as Sir Benjamin or as exotic as Sir Edmund, but I do come from the Mullery line, which is Queen Bethany's own line. Certainly that should impress you some." He laughed and offered his arm. "Allow me to escort you through the King's gardens."

The other two knights scowled at him. They didn't like that he asked before they did. Had they not been so polite, waiting for all introductions to be made, then they could have been leading Grace through the gardens instead.

Grace wanted nothing more than to head into her room and get some rest before her own nightly activities began. However, she didn't want to be rude and disgrace her cousin's name by refusing a relation to the queen. She took the offered arm and Tristan led her into the King's garden. As she moved away from Benjamin and Edmund, she smiled at them. They both returned the smile to show they had no hard feelings toward her, though they scowled at Tristan's back.

Outside, other couples made use of the quiet garden to make declarations of undying love, while others were engaged in less appropriate behaviors in the shadows. Grace often wondered what such things would be like, but in Arganis men saw her as a feisty youth and not as a court-able young woman. That suited her fine most days, but her Uncle George felt that at seventeen, she should already have had several marriage proposals. That's why he insisted, as did Uncle Leon, that she needed to go to the tournament. They hoped she'd be snatched up by a worthy noble family and a marriage proposal would follow sometime in the summer months. Grace did not like this prospect, and shivered to think of herself as a wife in the next year.

Again, Tristan misread the signals her body sent and wrapped his arm around her shoulder. "I would think a northern lady such as yourself would not find Ursana cold, especially since summer is on our doorstep."

She looked up into Tristan's face. He had a gift for misunderstanding her. Still, she smiled at him. As a man, he couldn't understand how she felt. Old men could marry, but not old women. Men only knew the pressure of finding a fertile wife or risking the end of their blood line. Grace would have been happy to not bear children to a man for the sake of a name. These thoughts ran unbidden across the fields of her mind as she walked through the garden, while Tristan talked on and on about his exploits; unaware his walking partner wasn't absorbing even a single word.

"I heard a nasty rumor you were planning to leave after the tournament ends." Grace escaped her mental fields to return to the palace's garden path. "Did no one tell of the wonderful festivals King Frederick holds here in the summer? The tournament is not the only attraction. Dancers, feasts, the market where sellers from across the country set up stalls. The city and the palace become alive. Besides, many young women find husbands during these times."

"I have heard of these things, and my uncles like to remind me that I am older than a fair number of married girls. They also warned me engagements can be very short during the tournament season if the families feel it is a fruitful match." She stressed the word "warned." In truth, Leon hadn't so much warned her as he insisted she project herself in such a way as to ensure a proposal by summer's end. She once heard him speaking to George that if she did not get an offer by eighteen, they may as well send her to the Temple of Kamaria to become a priestess. That was the fate of many unwed women.

"Aye, that is how my father and mother came to be married. They came together from an instant and mutual attraction. It happens often during the tournament season." Grace was all too aware of Tristan moving closer as he spoke. He also stopped their walk. "I believe I can understand such a thing; can you?"

Grace attempted to step away from Tristan's grasp, but he held her close. "I should be going," she whispered.

Tristan turned her so she was completely facing him. He stood a full head taller than she and he had her by the shoulders, holding fast, with a playful smile on his lips. Suddenly, he pulled her into a kiss.

Grace had sneaked into the stables before and stolen kisses from the young men who tended the horses in Arganis, but they were just simple pecks, not totally encompassing kisses like the one she now found herself in. Moments passed; too swiftly and yet too slowly at the same time. She broke away finally, feeling dazed at Tristan's bluntness. Her cheeks were deep crimson and she felt them getting hot. He was handsome, but such kisses didn't belong to a stranger like him. Her cheeks started to flush from anger and embarrassment. She liked this man well enough, however this was not something she was used to.

"You are a bashful maiden, aren't you?" Tristan held out his arm again for her. "I will escort you to your room, my lady."

~*~*~

Tristan stole several more kisses as he walked her back, and Grace didn't know how to tactfully stop him. Her attempts to pull away were misinterpreted as bashful maiden behavior. However, the more kisses he gave to her, the more she wanted them. Still, she felt quite lucky to see Cassandra waiting outside her chambers for her. Her hard stare stopped Tristan from trying any more.

Once Grace was shuffled into her chambers, Cassandra sat her on the bed. "He's quite a handsome young man."

Cassandra wanted information. Her angry stare was only a show so she could get rid of Tristan faster. Now with the door closed, she was excited to see what Grace had to say.

"He kissed me in the gardens, quite passionately." Cassandra put her hands to her mouth. She was thrilled; Grace could see it in her eyes. "Is that proper behavior here? In Arganis, Leon would skin a boy for trying that with me."

"Things are different at home. Leon is very conservative in any and all romantic aspects, and George never notices these things. Just don't get yourself caught, because innocent garden kisses can ruin a reputation if the wrong eyes should see."

"Eyes that belong to Katherine of Actis?"

Cassandra tapped the side of her nose. "I heard you had an encounter with a snake at dinner." Grace raised her eyebrow. "Calvin came looking for you only a few moments before your return. You need to watch out for that woman." As Cassandra spoke, she slowly pulled things from Grace's trunk.

Leather jerkin, black riding trousers, a black, long-sleeved tunic, old leather riding boots, and an executioner's hood. All were laid out before Grace on the bed. The hood stared up at its master with blank eyes. "We've the fortune of being placed on the first floor, milady." Cassandra now set to work helping Grace undress. "The only flaw, of course, is that a watchman makes his rounds in the area and passes the window every half hour. He passed this room ten minutes ago. I've been watching him all night. If you insist on going out, let me extinguish the lights and we'll wait for his next pass."

Cassandra was a homebody. Her life, as she and everyone else saw it, was to sew, cook, and clean up after the women of the Hilren line. Her mother was a maid, her maternal grandmother was a seamstress, and her paternal grandmother was a cook. The Cooper women had never lived exciting lives, so for the young maid, it was exciting that the lady she waited on was adventurous. Grace felt she needed the careful organization of Cassandra to go about at night, and Cassandra made sure the coast was clear while Grace used this knowledge to sneak around. When Grace was ready, Cassandra extinguished the flames. She would sit and wait for the hour to get later before going out.

Three

Grace went out sometime after the night watch rang the first hour. By that time, she believed it would be safe to venture out somewhat unseen. She took a quick nap after Tristan returned her to her room, and when she awoke at midnight there were still a few courtiers making merry around the palace. By one o'clock, almost the whole ground had fallen silent. No doubt many knights were resting their bodies for the first day of the tournament, and none wanted to be too bogged down with good food and wine.

Sneaking out was no simple task, but dressed in black, she managed to avoid detection. The clouds were in her favor that night; blocking the moonlight from the paths and making her unseen to the castle guards. Just before sunrise, hooded and cloaked, Grace crept back into her room. Caked in mud, she threw herself down on her bed and fell into a deep sleep.

A few hours later Cassandra threw open the shutters of the room and Grace groaned as she was forced out of her sleep. Her servant stood over her bed, wearing a scowl that could curdle milk. Grace pulled the covers up and over her head. It was hot under the blankets, but she wasn't ready to face the day yet.

"Up," Cassandra said, and pulled the sheets from Grace. "You will be late again if you do not get up now."

"Who cares?" Grace mumbled, and covered her head with the pillow since her blankets had been taken.

"I do. It is bad form to miss the first day of the tournament, especially the blessing of the knights ceremony. Now get up. We have to clean you up before you make an appearance. The temple priests will not be so pleased if you wander into the service late and dirty, and I'll not have people thinking you have a bad maid who can't even make you look presentable."

Grace sat up in her bed and looked down at herself. Before dropping off to sleep, she only managed to get her hood off. She still wore the jerkin and breeches, and her riding boots had left muddy prints on the sheets. She could feel bits of mud stuck to her face and dirt was under her fingernails, but it did not bother

29

her. Cassandra, on the other hand, was not so complacent about her appearance. The maid accepted her choice in life, but she didn't accept the mess it made.

"I can go to the tournament like this," Grace said, though she regretted the words the moment they released themselves from her tongue.

Cassandra's face turned ghostly white and then bright red in a matter of seconds. "Do not even joke about that! If anyone in court were to discover you were the—" She paused; not wanting to risk anyone overhearing her.

"You would be hanged straight away. You know how the old men of this court feel about women doing what they deem *men's work*. They look down upon women in other countries who rule their lands. They whisper that women like that should be flogged, or worse. And what about those who firmly disapprove of enforcement of the law being taken up by a random citizen? What you do is even worse than just holding lands; it's against the law, and while a man might get away with it, you won't. Please, Grace, do not joke about such things."

Cassandra was only half right in her beliefs. Men like King Frederick did not wholly hate or fear women, or peasants for that matter, who were smart or strong. Rather, he hated and feared those who were not men of noble birth, but who proved themselves more adept than the noblemen. The nobles were the rulers, the lawmakers, the knights; if women and peasants could outsmart them, pride and honor were hurt. Still, the image projected was one of hate toward them in all cases. That was why Grace couldn't become the Lady of Barony Arganis unless she married a lesser son of a greater house. Even then, Arganis would be her husband's house, not the Hilren's.

The young woman knew Cassandra was right. Frederick would not think twice about having her punished. The work she did was already considered outside the law, but Frederick allowed her brand of justice to continue for whatever reason. If he discovered it was a woman out at night, he would throw her in a dungeon, or worse. Grace got out of bed and followed all of

Cassandra's instructions so she would look presentable for the court.

~*~*~

The temple of the sun god, Ciro, was flooded with people. It was a grand place; there was no mistaking that. Grace had never been somewhere so lavish. Behind the altar was a large, golden statue of the sun god himself. Ciro's left hand was held out, while his right hand was on his breast. Bright summer flowers were wreathed around his head, and Grace guessed the wives, daughters or mothers of the competing knights decorated the god's statue to bring good luck to the men. She remembered wreathing the statue of Ciro in Arganis when Calvin ventured to gain his shield, and assumed things would be no different here.

The knights who were to compete knelt before the altar while the priests chanted and put Ciro's blessing upon them. The sun god would bestow good fortune onto the tournament and those who competed. At the end of the day, they would do the same for Kamaria, Ciro's sister, in the moon goddess's temple. It was all to ensure no one was hurt during the tournament.

Grace watched as her cousin was blessed. She felt odd and out of place in the temple, because again, everyone was dressed more lavishly than she. Even the temple itself was; with the gold surfaces shimmering in the sun that shone through the great temple windows. Clearly the priests of Ursana were not in need of vast donations for their holy house. The temple around Arganis was in constant need of repairs, and its statues of the Divine Twins, Ciro and Kamaria, were made of wood. Her uncle George didn't see much need in decorating Ciro with vast amounts of gold, not when such money could be put to better use elsewhere. He was by no means blasphemous to the god and goddess; rather George was a practical man, and Grace understood his desire to see the people fed before outfitting the temple with gold.

Grace sighed. She wanted to leave. Worshipping was not supposed to be so luxurious, it was supposed to be for reflection and deep thought. She missed her temple at home; a peaceful place with few distractions. Grace was happy when the priests

31

finished their blessings and everyone rose to leave.

~*~*~

It was not even noon yet and the sun was already beating down as people flooded in from all over to see the tournament. The poor, the merchants and the nobles all gathered for the opening day, and Grace found herself swept up in the excitement of the atmosphere. These sorts of things did not happen in Arganis. The most exciting times were the days after harvest when the villagers gathered at the castle. Leon provided a feast, and George thanked those who helped make Arganis prosperous. But that celebration of good health was nothing compared to what King Frederick held in Ursana.

More spectators turned out for the tournament than there were people in Arganis. She vaguely remembered the crowds from when she came as a girl, but memories did not prepare her for all the activity. She arrived with several other court ladies, and only caught a glimpse of the market where commoners from all over Cesernan gathered to sell goods and services. Grace was far more interested in that, but Cassandra was trying fervently to keep her out of trouble so she would have to come back and explore later.

"Grace, my dear!" Henry's robust voice brought a smile to her face. He was already seated in the stadium in front of the jousting ring. "Sit here with me. I saved you a seat."

Grace lifted her skirts and climbed the few stairs to take a seat next to Henry. He rose and bowed to her, as was custom. He even took her hand and gave it a gentle kiss.

"I thought you would rather not be seated next to the ladies who follow Katherine's word as though it were law. Besides, we did have a lovely conversation last night at the feast. I hope we can continue it."

"You are a good friend to me," Grace said. "And far better company than anyone else I have met." Her thoughts went to Tristan's kiss and she hid a blush. "Tell me, how will the jousting go? Calvin is to compete today and I do not want to miss him, but I had hoped to see a few rounds of the sword fighting."

32

"Sword fighting, eh? Not many nobles make their way down there, unless of course Prince Drake is competing. They think too many commoners and lesser knights compete. But I will walk down there with you after the first round of jousting. I once took part in the sword fighting myself, though it has been many long, food-filled years since then." Henry patted his large stomach. "As for jousting, the lesser knights – the knights without a claim to any real plots of land – will go first in all the events. Calvin will not compete until sometime after lunch."

Grace nodded. "Calvin is competing in the sword fighting as well, but he is not to go until tomorrow. I would very much like to see how other knights compare to my cousin."

Henry laughed and patted Grace's shoulder. "Few women of the court take any interest in this. They care about the joust and who wins that. It is usually Sir Benjamin of Salatia, and then the young ladies lobby for his attention." Henry sighed. "It was not always so. Knights from other countries used to come to compete, but most knights now are too young to remember such times."

"What happened to the tournament? My Uncle Leon used to talk of its grandeur not being matched anywhere else in the world." Grace had limited knowledge of the countries around Cesernan. Most were just names to her. She could name their kings and queens and point to them on a map, but nothing else. George tried to teach her, but she was always more interested in what Leon was teaching. She could read and write, but that was the furthest George ever got with her. Mathematics, geography, history…all those subjects bored her to tears.

Henry looked around and lowered his voice. "Years ago, the kingdom of Sera sent their knights, as did Eurur and Archon. It was a longstanding tradition to halt border disputes and wars to come to Cesernan for the annual tournament. This lasted for over a century." Grace nodded, because she had heard all this before. Sera and Archon were neighboring countries, and the country of Eurur was separated by the sea. The idea was to foster fellowship by extending the tournament invitation to other countries, in order to cultivate peace and understanding.

Henry continued, "The knights from Sera were so well trained, they put many of our men to shame. You see, they have often focused their energies on building an army with no rival. This is because Sera has always had border problems. When King Philip died in a skirmish along his borders, his only child took the throne at fifteen.

"Princess Elanor of Sera fought alongside her father for years as a squire and page. She was a fine warrior, though still fairly green. But since taking the throne, she hasn't yet married. It never sat right with King Frederick, and others from outside Cesernan agreed. What kind of country allowed a woman to inherit such a tract of land? People asked this over and over. The first tournament after Elanor was crowned Queen, she came to Cesernan with five of her finest knights. It was made very clear that she was disapproved of, and her knights would not advance in the tournament, no matter how exceptional their skills were. That was nigh on fifteen years ago. After Sera withdrew, Eurur followed. They would not compete if their friends in Sera did not. Archon stayed for a few more years, but found the competition lacking without the other two. It is a shame, really. I would like to see those knights return to the tournament before I die." Henry fell silent and hung his head. "But Frederick is stubborn and upholds the tradition and biases of his father. I suppose I cannot blame him for that. He is mired in tradition, but aren't we all?"

Grace listened with wide eyes and was amazed at Henry's tale. She knew Sera had a queen and no king, but the bias Elanor met with was a new piece of the tale. She found it hard to believe such a woman could exist in this world. Queen Elanor openly defied generations of tradition by not marrying and not submitting to a husband's rule. Not only that, she was a trained warrior. Grace would have loved to see the Queen openly defy the men of her country by refusing to marry and submit.

If Grace had listened more carefully to George's teachings, she would have understood that what was uncommon for Cesernan was not so uncommon in Sera. Elanor wasn't breaking tradition, because hers were a proud, willful people who valued courage and honor above anything else in their leaders. To them no one, not even the beloved King Philip, embodied these ideals better than Elanor. However, the image of the warrior Queen provided inspiration to Grace for a long time after hearing Henry's story. That fact alone was more important than the truth behind the matter.

~*~*~

Henry and Grace watched the first round of the joust before heading to the sword fighting ring. A few lesser nobles were watching, but no one of high status had come to see the competition. The two watched as Sir Gerald and Sir Tomas squared off in the ring.

"I say Tomas wins," Grace whispered to Henry as the two men began circling each other.

"Oh? Everyone else thinks Gerald will win this round. He is the more seasoned knight, and has become renowned among the lesser nobles as a fine swordsman. He's taken first in the sword at least five, maybe even six times. What makes you say Tomas?"

"It is in their stances. Gerald watches his face, but Tomas watches his body movement to try and predict Gerald's next maneuver. And look how Tomas moves his feet; he has excellent balance. Besides, Gerald thinks he has nothing to fear. He has won this tournament before, and Tomas is too new to have won much of anything. Arrogance against a smaller, less experienced opponent is often the downfall of the strongest. Just watch – Tomas will win."

The crowds cheered as the two knights clashed swords. Henry watched their movements with great interest. Tomas seemed to dance around Gerald, who stayed flatfooted and used his upper body more than his legs. The two threw themselves at one another again and again. Tomas caught Gerald under his sword arm, quickly disarmed him and put his own sword to Gerald's throat. He had won.

Henry looked at Grace carefully. She did not look at him, but wore a smug smile on her face as Tomas was declared the victor. Henry was amazed the young woman had successfully named the winner and accurately critiqued their fighting styles. Most third year pages wouldn't have been able to do that.

"Know much about swordplay?"

Grace blushed a little. "Arganis has been subjected to bandits and pirates in the past. My Uncle Leon wanted to make sure I was safe, and so I learned a little bit of the sword while Calvin trained for his shield."

Henry nodded to make Grace believe he was satisfied with her response, but she had a little more than just 'basic' knowledge of the fighting. He could tell she was holding back. It was easy to teach swordplay, but it took interest on a pupil's part to invest much into critiquing others. Henry hoped she never started such a conversation with anyone else in court. Though the men found her beautiful now, no one would want a wife who could tell him what he was doing wrong with his weapons. Henry would have to probe Grace more, though. He didn't mind conversing on the subject with such a bright young lady.

~*~*~

The Death Dealer hid in the shadows along the side of the road. Word spread fast that The Death Dealer was in Ursana, so only a few bold criminals came out. So far, Grace had already stopped two roadside robberies. She needed only to emerge from the shadows and the men set off running. That was a favorable response, but also a boring one. It was nice to have a challenge once in a while.

Footfalls filled Grace's ears. People were approaching.

"We'll make them pay for what they did. No one throws lamp oil on one of my men," a gruff voice whispered in the dark. Grace squatted down and gripped her sword hilt.

"What about The Death Dealer? They say he's in Ursana. He could be protecting Wilson and his family. There are plenty of families to steal from in other places. Let's just go."

"No one bests me or my men, you coward." Grace saw the larger man hit his companion across the back of the head. "I'm not scared of a little boy wearing a hood and playing with a sword. We're going to do what we set out to do."

Grace stepped into their path and both men stopped. The smaller one, the one who was afraid of The Death Dealer, looked at his boss and took off running the way they had come.

"Damn coward. Well, I guess it's just you and me. You don't look so strong, boy. How about I let you run, and I'll not say a word?" Grace held her ground and unsheathed her sword to show him she wasn't going to turn tail and run. The man let out a primal yell and lunged at Grace.

Thrown off guard, she stumbled backwards against the force of the man's body. Grace had never encountered someone who jumped into a fight like this. Many people she stood against hesitated a little, and she relied on that hesitation to ready herself for a fight; to move first. She made to slice at him with her sword, but he hit her with the full force of his body before she was ready. The larger man was suddenly on top of her and he gave her a few solid punches in the gut, as well as a few to her face. He knocked the sword clear from her hand. Grace squirmed underneath him and bit his knuckles as he tried to punch her face again. She was lucky the impact didn't break any of her teeth, and for all the effort, she only managed to peel away some of the skin on his knuckles.

"You whelp!" he screamed and held Grace down. His hand reached down and produced a dagger. "Not so tough without your little sword are you?" He pinned her down and taunted her with the dagger. "How to start with ya...how to start...?"

Grace took a deep breath. With every bit of strength she had, she flung her head forward and made contact with the man's nose. There was a loud crack, he squeaked once, and then fell on top of her heavily. Blood rushed from his nose into Grace's face as she struggled to get him off of her. Her Uncle Leon once told her that if she was unarmed and in grave danger, the best thing to do was go for the nose. He stated often times it would end in a broken nose, but on rare occasions and with the right amount of force, it could end in death.

Grace's hit forced the man's nasal bones into his brain and he died instantly. Now she had no idea what to do. She sat by the body and shook over the gravity of what she had just done. There was a rush running through her body, but it wasn't fear; it was something else. She had no idea how long she sat there, but finally Grace dragged herself to her feet and set off running for the castle. By the time she climbed back into her room, the adrenaline wore off and she crashed.

~*~*~

Cassandra entered Grace's chambers early the next morning, when the sun barely began to show itself to the world. She was still in bed with the covers drawn over her face. "You complain about this heat and here you are, wrapped up in those blankets like it was about to start snowing. Now get up and let's get you ready for the tournament. You do not want to miss Calvin in the sword competition today."

"I am not going," Grace muttered from under the blankets. "Tell everyone I am ill."

"Of course you are going! Now get up." Cassandra pulled the covers clear off Grace. She yelped a little and quickly clapped a hand over her own mouth.

Grace's face was covered in dried blood, the entire right side of her face was one blue and purple bruise, and her right eye was swollen shut. Grace let out a pained whimper and lifted up her jerkin a bit. Her midsection was covered in the same kinds of bruises.

"All the blood—" Cassandra could hardly find the words. Her voice became nothing more than a raspy whisper.

"It is not mine. The man...he pulled a dagger. I had to kill him. He just bled all over me and stared at me with these unseeing eyes." The memory rushed back like a flood. Those eyes would always have the look of surprise in them.

Cassandra sat on the bed next to Grace and took her hand. "You? You killed him?"

Grace nodded and her servant looked aghast. How could she explain to her friend that there was barely any regret for killing a man who was going to harm an entire family? She felt remorse for ending another's life, but not so much knowing she helped a

38

family escape his wrath. Not to mention the fact that he intended to kill her. Cassandra would never understand, but then again, Grace barely understood it herself. After fleeing from the body, she vomited along the side of the road. She killed a man. Trying to justify all the reasons she felt guilty and all the reasons she didn't caused her a headache. She shivered and Cassandra held her fast.

The maid stroked her hair. "He'd have killed you," was all she said.

Grace didn't want to ever feel like this again. Next time a man pulled a knife on her, she'd knock him unconscious and tie him to a tree. Killing again was not an option. Her stomach churned at the thought. And to think earlier that evening she found scaring brigands off boring. She would take boring over the alternative now.

"You cannot just stay in bed all day. Word will get out that The Death Dealer has killed, and when you suddenly do not show up, people will talk. No – you have to go out." Grace wanted to roll her eyes. Cassandra was playing the fatalist. No one would put those pieces together. However, Grace knew her maid would be on edge all day with paranoia if she didn't go out. A nervous Cassandra was a greater danger to her than someone figuring out who The Death Dealer was.

Cassandra rooted through Grace's things until she found her riding tunic and gown. She ripped bits and pieces off of it and wiped Grace's face with the rest. "We will take you to the healer, say you were on a ride last night and were thrown into a ditch."

"What if the stable hands are questioned?"

"A few pieces of silver will get them to say anything you like. Hurry up and get dressed and then it is off to the healer with you."

~*~*~

Calvin's manservant and Grace's friend, Donald, went to the stables to talk with the stable hands about Grace's "fall." The stable hands did not question Donald or his need for them to lie. They assumed only that this young Grace woman had spoken out

39

of turn and a male relative put her in her place, and now the family was trying to cover it up. These things weren't all that uncommon. Plenty of other court ladies had suffered from "falls" in the past. While Donald handled one situation, Cassandra took Grace to see the castle healer to handle another.

He was an old man who looked as though he had lived through every king of Cesernan. He grabbed Grace's face with his icy hands and she was reminded of death, which brought up the image of those dead eyes again. Her heart beat faster. The healer moved her head this way and that, looking over her bruises carefully.

"You should have come to me last night when your horse threw you. I could have stopped the swelling on your eye." He released her face and walked to a cabinet.

"I did not want to inconvenience you since all your candles were already out. I had no idea I would wake up looking like this."

He mumbled to himself as he looked about his cabinets. "When I was young, ladies didn't go riding after dark. Probably went to meet a lover." Grace rolled her eyes. The healer turned back to her, holding a small blue bottle. "Take this ointment, apply to your eye every few hours, and by tomorrow the swelling should go down. There's nothing I can do for those bruises, but in a few days they won't be as bad." He handed her the ointment. "You are very lucky to have survived with only a few bruises. I suggest having something done with the horse you were riding."

"Thank you, sir." She curtsied and left his room.

Cassandra was waiting for her. "Well?"

"I do not see why I cannot stay in bed. No one will suspect a thing. You are being paranoid about this."

"I refuse to take a risk." Cassandra took Grace by the arm and started to lead her down the hall. "I will do nothing that could possibly put you in the hangman's sight. You will do as the healer said and you will go to the tournament today. I am going to see how Donald fared with the stable boys. Meanwhile, you stay out of trouble." Cassandra patted Grace's shoulder and was gone.

Grace looked at the blue bottle and sighed. She should have stayed in Arganis. The healer in Arganis wouldn't have believed she was off seeing a lover. He'd have scolded her about proper riding techniques and handed over the ointment with a laugh and a smile.

"I, for one, would like to see how Benjamin fares today against Calvin." Grace heard voices down the hall. She looked around for a place to hide, but all the doors near her were closed and she didn't want to discover what was behind them simply to escape conversation. Instead she walked toward the voices; head high, bruises showing proudly.

To her surprise, Prince Drake and Sir Tristan of Escion rounded the corner and the three came face to face.

"Good morning, Grace," Drake said and bowed to her. "My dear lady, what happened to your lovely face?"

"I was thrown from my horse last night, although it is really not as bad as it looks."

"Thrown from your horse?" Tristan said. "Then certainly the beast is not worthy to bear you. Escion is known for breeding the most noble of horses. If it pleases the lady, perhaps I could arrange for a nobler animal for you?" The young knight was looking for any morsel she would throw him. She was able to avoid him the day before, but there was no avoiding him now.

Drake cut in, saying, "Why go to Escion for a horse when the King's horses are by far the greatest in the kingdom? We have plenty for you here in Ursana that my father will gladly give away as a present to one so fair."

Grace saw exactly what the knights were doing and found the spectacle rather amusing. The men in Arganis saw her as simply Grace; a pleasant girl who was their friend, as well as the only child of their old lord. She was no prize for them. Watching Tristan and Drake vie for her attention and affection was something new for her, but she could not say it was completely unwanted, especially after the way Katherine snubbed her. Forgetting what happened the night before, Grace's mind returned to Drake's dancing and Tristan's kisses.

Both were handsome, prize-winning knights. Drake was lean and tall, with black hair that hung into his brown eyes. He had a friendly face and she had yet to see him frown. Tristan was equally as lean, but a bit shorter. He let his brown hair grow out a bit longer, yet he was not nearly as friendly-looking as Drake...he had a serious air about him. Grace respected both men as fighters and wondered what they saw in her.

Grace fought back a bit of laughter and composed herself. "My poor horse is a noble animal who was spooked. There is no need to replace her."

"If the lady insists," Drake said. "Allow me to escort you to the jousting for the day. Your cousin is in the first round against the 'unbeatable' Sir Benjamin of Salatia. I am sure you do not want to miss that."

Tristan cleared his throat. "But Drake, you are expected for the first round in the archery tournament today. You mustn't be late. I will escort Lady Grace to the jousting."

Grace saw Drake clench his hands, but the smile never left his face. "Right you are, Tristan." He bowed to Grace. "I shall see you later, my lady." He stalked away; clenching and unclenching his fists.

"Shall we?" Tristan held out his arm and Grace gratefully took it.

"First I must change and put this ointment on."

"Of course." Tristan led her toward the guest wing. "I had hoped to see you yesterday, but it appeared that old man had all your time to himself. That is most unfair to those of us who are young and looking to court."

Grace avoided his eyes. She didn't dislike his attentions, and admittedly he was a handsome man. All the games of the high court world in Ursana were still new to her, though. Succumbing to feelings that weren't genuine seemed unwise and potentially heartbreaking later. Still, she had no way of knowing how young knights such as Tristan felt about these sorts of things. So rather than sharing her true feelings she only said, "He is a seasoned knight and can shed light on all the traditions and rules of the tournament."

"Yes, Henry certainly is a learned man. But please, allow me to entertain you today, even if it be alongside Henry. For you see, Grace, I am quite taken by your beauty, your gift of shyness and of course, your quiet nature. It would break my heart to not spend as many of my waking minutes as possible with you."

Tristan stopped walking and turned Grace to face him as he spoke all these words. Flattery…what a strange beast. She searched his face for any signs of insincerity and saw none, but there was a certain hardness and stubbornness in his face. Undecided on Tristan's exact motives, Grace permitted him to kiss her cheek.

"Afraid someone will catch us?" he asked; resuming their walk.

"A reputation is easy to destroy, good sir," was all Grace said in return, though she was not concerned with that at the moment. She was more interested in understanding Tristan and the feelings he claimed to have for her.

~*~*~

Grace arrived on Tristan's arm to the jousting ring and scanned the crowds for Henry. A day alone in the company of Tristan was a daunting task, as the young knight didn't seem concerned about being caught and judged by other nobles. Grace, however, still cared and had no interest in becoming more of a social pariah than she already was. Her search for a chaperone was not in vain. She spotted Henry waving to her from the second row of seats.

"There is Henry of Egona. Let us sit by him."

"As the lady wishes." Tristan led Grace up to sit by Henry.

Henry was shocked to see Grace with Tristan. He hoped she would not get involved with the knights of the court. He respected her because she was different from most of the women who turned out for the tournament, but seeing her with Tristan made him sigh inwardly. He feared if she grew fond of a knight like Tristan, and he fond of her in return, then Katherine would easily sink her talons into Grace. He tried to hide his worried face from

Grace as she came toward him. No use fretting over something that hadn't yet come to pass. "Grace dear, have you and Tristan come to join me? Please sit, children."

Grace took a seat between Tristan and Henry.

"Child, I saw your cousin's manservant, Donald this morning in the stables. He told me about the accident with your horse. I do hope you are all right. It is not nearly as bad as I feared. The way Donald went on, I thought all the bones were broken in your body." Henry touched one of her bruises gently and then patted her hand. "Though those bruises hide your beauty."

"Yes, it is not as serious as Cassandra and Donald are making it out to be; just a scratch."

Henry patted her hand lightly again and turned his attention to the ring. "This is going to be an excellent match. Calvin is a real natural at jousting, and Benjamin is one of the King's best. You should be proud to have your cousin competing against a valiant champion such as Benjamin."

"I am proud of him." Grace paused. "Yet I worry for Calvin at the same time."

"Why is that?" Henry asked; his face jovial and his manner merry. Grace wished hers was the same.

"Have you ever killed anyone, Henry?" Both Henry and Tristan stared at Grace. Nothing could have prepared them for the question she laid before them. Knowing an explanation was needed, she continued. "I ask only because one day, my dear, sweet cousin could go to war, and he may kill or be killed upon a battlefield. I wanted to know, from a seasoned knight, what is waiting for my cousin."

"Child..." Henry touched her cheek softly as a father would. "Do you worry no one will mourn Calvin? Obviously you and your kin will, but you should not trouble your mind with these thoughts. They are dark and dreary for this beautiful day Ciro has blessed us with."

"The tournament brings to mind thoughts of war. I want to know what sort of pain my cousin will go through if he should have to kill. Can there be remorse for killing an enemy?" Grace truly did wonder about what would happen should Calvin go to war, but now she only wanted absolution for what happened to her in the dark watches of the night.

"What silly questions, girl!" Tristan attempted a laugh, but a stern look from Henry stopped him.

"As a knight of this realm, you too should be asking these morality questions, boy," Henry said. He took hold of Grace's hands. "When I was twenty, I went to the Nareroc Islands to help quell an uprising. My squire, who was months from earning his shield, was along. An island native nearly killed him when we were taking the night watch over our camp. To save my squire, I slew the man. He was the first man I ever killed. At the time, I told myself he was the enemy and I was right in my action. But as the years have gone by, I think of the man from time to time and wonder who mourned him, and if my action changed their lives. I saved a friend's life by ending another's. Sometimes those are the choices before soldiers; to kill in order to save. Should Calvin see war, this will be before him." Henry forced a smile, though it was a sad one. "Right or wrong, I did what I felt I had to, and no more can be asked of any man. Is your mind somewhat eased?"

Grace nodded. For right or wrong, she snuffed out the life of a man who threatened someone else. Like Henry, she would now carry the memory until the end of her days.

Tristan said, "The match is about to begin. I, for one, would like to end this most depressing of conversations while the world laughs around us."

"Yes!" Henry laughed. "Whole months are dedicated to death and dying. Let us enjoy these days of merrymaking!"

As Henry turned his attention away, Tristan slipped his hand over Grace's. Grace looked at him with raised eyebrows, but Tristan was looking toward the ring where Calvin and Benjamin appeared at opposite ends. Tristan acted as though this was normal. It didn't feel normal, but Grace said nothing in objection. Strange as it was, it wasn't unpleasant.

She turned her attention to the ring; forgetting Tristan's hand. The herald announced the knights and the two made ready. Grace inhaled deeply and sat upright. This was an important match for Calvin. She had heard from her uncles that a knight's standing could easily be determined in his first tournament. So far Calvin had won his matches in the joust and sword, but he also competed against lesser noble families and other newcomers to the tournament. A match against Benjamin would show the people what he was really capable of. If he was able to break Benjamin's lance and score a few points, it wouldn't matter if he lost. It could possibly show that Calvin was able to hold his own, even with legends like Sir Benjamin of Salatia.

She watched anxiously as the flag went down, the horses charged forward and the lances were lowered. Every second that ticked by took an eternity, until there was a crash and Benjamin's lance made contact with Calvin's right shoulder. A point for Benjamin. This meant nothing; Calvin still had a chance to recover and get a point on the other knight.

Again they squared off across the ring. The flag went down and the horses charged once more. Grace watched in slow motion as Calvin's lance hit Benjamin squarely in the chest with a loud crash. Everything moved far too quickly after that. The next thing Grace saw was Benjamin lying flat on his back and the crowds cheering. Calvin had just unhorsed the finest jouster in the kingdom. Calvin won. All the people were cheering; amazed someone finally unhorsed the famous Benjamin.

Grace jumped from her seat; lightheaded with delight. "I have to go see him."

"I'll take you down to him," Tristan said; taking Grace by the hand and leading her off to where the knights were.

Grace could barely speak. Her excitement was overflowing and it seemed to take forever to walk to see Calvin. It took even longer when Tristan stopped her; pulling her aside as they moved through the stables toward the knights' area.

"Your cousin did well. No one has unhorsed Benjamin since his first tournament."

"I knew he could do it. Calvin has been training his whole life."

Tristan nodded and suddenly, with no warning, pulled Grace into a kiss. It only lasted a moment, but felt a good deal longer to Grace. Tristan pulled away and continued to lead Grace over to where Calvin was. She was as breathless and shocked as the first time he kissed her. Were these things normal in the court? The boys who stole kisses in Arganis did so after much hand-holding and blushing. It was never so quick or treated like it happened all the time. Tristan looked back to Grace and winked, and stopped her three more times before reaching Calvin to get a kiss.

However, once she saw Calvin she forgot about Tristan's kisses and rushed at her cousin to throw her arms around him. He hugged back with his left arm. Grace pulled away and moved to hug Donald. It was a bit of his victory as well.

"Grace, will you be joining us at the sword fighting ring? Calvin is to fight there in less than ten minutes."

"Would I miss seeing Calvin win again? Of course I will join you." She turned to Tristan. "Will you join us?"

"I am afraid not. I have my own jousting match soon." He gave Grace a peck on the cheek. "But we shall see each other later."

Grace blushed, knowing Calvin and Donald were staring intently. The boys she grew up with were not used to seeing Grace being fawned over by men. "I do believe our young Grace is becoming a woman," Calvin said with a laugh, and then he and Donald started toward the sword fighting ring. Grace trailed them, scowling a bit; knowing they would never let up on the teasing.

~*~*~

Calvin was fighting against Tomas. The knight who Grace saw win the day before had advanced far, and proved to be a worthy opponent. Grace had no doubt of her cousin's victory, though. The knights stepped into the ring and then it hit Grace: Calvin was not going to win this time.

He held his sword in his left hand. He was taught how to fight with both hands, but his right was dominant. It puzzled Grace why Calvin would switch sword hands now. She looked at his right arm and saw that it hung helplessly at his side. The fight began and Grace knew it was already lost for Calvin.

Calvin's right arm became dead weight and he could not use it even to block. Grace looked away to spare herself from watching Calvin lose. The fight ended quickly and Calvin stormed from the ring. He was far enough ahead in the sword to stay within the tournament, but he would need to win his next match to stay in. His next match was scheduled in half an hour. Grace and Donald followed him closely all the way back to his chambers.

~*~*~

Calvin sat on his bed in his breeches and riding boots while Grace tended to his shoulder. There was little she could do. Cassandra was ready with a bowl of warm water and a rag for them.

"Benjamin's lance hit a weak spot in my armor. I felt my shoulder shift, and now it's useless."

"You need to go see the healer," Donald said. His blue eyes were filled with concern as he looked at Calvin.

"Your shoulder is not beyond repair, Calvin." Grace helped Calvin off his bed. "If we have you tended now, you'll be as good as new in a few days."

"I will have to withdraw from the next round of the sword. I am supposed to duel against Prince Drake in fifteen minutes. I will tell the herald I must forfeit, and then I will go to the healer."

"No, you see the healer first. Donald and I will go to the herald for you." Grace looked at Cassandra. "Can you take him to the castle healer?"

"Of course. Come on, Calvin. You will be good as new before you know it, and next year you will be able to win in the joust *and* the sword." Cassandra helped Calvin to his feet and led him from the room; chattering happily about the glory he would gain the next year.

When Cassandra and Calvin left the chambers, Donald sighed. "I guess it's best if we do this now."

Grace looked at Donald and shook her head. "Donald, help

me into Calvin's armor."

Four

It was sweltering in the armor, especially since Grace had to wear extra clothing to make Calvin's armor less loose on her body. It helped a bit, but for the most part it made her sweat uncontrollably and even hampered her movements. Her biggest fear was the two inches in height she lacked that Calvin possessed. If anyone noticed this height difference, she would be in a great deal of trouble. So far, the people she and Donald walked by only noticed the coat of arms Grace bore on Calvin's shield. She received many pats on the back for Calvin's recent triumph against Benjamin.

Beads of sweat trickled down her face, and although she desperately wanted to wipe them away, the helmet prevented her from doing so. She wondered how knights went to war in the summer with such garb. Barely fifteen minutes had passed since she got in the armor and she was ready to faint from the heat. To sit in this all day without sweating to death…that was a gift from the gods.

Grace strode alongside Donald to the sword fighting ring. The manservant had not even tried to stop her. She knew that Donald hated the thought of Arganis pulling out due to injury, especially after the absence of so many years. It felt too much like dishonor. Grace felt the same. The young manservant was confident Grace could fight in Calvin's stead. He had seen her duel before, and though she wasn't as well-trained as the knights, she could at least convince the crowd she was Calvin. If they could do that, win or lose, they could maintain Arganis's honor. Neither thought beyond the minutes spent in the ring. What would happen when it was confirmed Calvin was at the healer at the same time he was in the sword ring?

Donald stopped Grace on their side of the ring and handed Calvin's sword to her. She was unused to the heft of such a blade; the one she carried was smaller and lighter. She gave it a few test swings to get used to the feel of the armor, extra clothing, and sword and shield.

Donald moved closer so that only she could hear. "Prince Drake has only lost a few times, mostly to Sir Gerald and Sir Benjamin. I've seen him duel before and he's quite adept, but he moves early and hard. Let him strike first, early, and often. Block as much as you can before moving against him. He's more practiced with heavy swords and shield than you. If you attack first, you'll tire faster. With any luck, he's already worn out from his earlier matches this morning. He's had at least one duel in the sword and one joust today, and if I'm not mistaken even a round in archery." Grace raised an eyebrow no one could see under the helmet. This seemed like too many events for one man in a day. "The King likes his son to show the world he is the best at everything. Now, if you follow my instructions, with any luck he'll tire quickly."

Grace nodded. "I have seen him in the sword ring as well. Drake will not be easy to best, especially since my skills with this sword are none too good. They may be fine enough against untrained brutes, but this man is a knight of the realm."

"You don't need to win. Just see to it that Arganis doesn't forfeit in disgrace."

Grace had fought against Calvin for a few years, but when they did they were armed with wooden practice swords or short swords. She bested him enough times to be confident in her sword technique, but now she was being thrown into the ring with a knight whose proficiencies far outweighed her own.

She looked at Donald through the eye slits of her helmet. He nodded and patted her shoulder. The herald stood in the middle of the ring, and in a thundering voice spoke and announced Drake and "Calvin." The King, Queen, and Princess, along with many other important nobles, came down to witness the Prince in the sword fighting ring. A special podium had been set up so the royal family didn't have to crowd around like commoners to see. Everyone cheered as Grace and Drake stepped into the ring, but Grace was deaf to it all as she watched the armored figure of Drake from across the ring. They crossed swords and bowed to one another, and then the herald waved a flag and it began.

Donald watched anxiously as Grace blocked Drake's first blow. As he hoped, Drake was going to attack first and often. "Come on then, you yellow-bellied fop!" Drake taunted; following an old tradition of the sword ring.

The two circled each other; Drake taunting, Grace silent. Again, the prince moved to attack and brought his sword down toward Grace's head. She moved to catch the blade with her own, but Drake had her in a bad position. He bore down on her from overhead; forcing Grace to her knees. If Grace was smarter, she would have dodged rather than try to catch the blade. As Grace neared the ground, she rolled away and toward the corner of the ring where Donald stood watching.

"He hits like a hammer," she gasped. She was on her feet swiftly enough and dodged another blow from the Prince.

It was now Grace's turn to be on the offensive. With his next attack Drake showed he was slowing down; from the heat, if nothing else. Grace was no better, but her arms weren't as tired as the Prince's and she hadn't been competing for days. That made her fresh, even if the heat didn't. She lunged at the Prince. He was just fast enough to dodge, but not fast enough to stop her rapid second attack.

Something in the crowd caught Donald's eye and he was distracted from the action in the ring. Grace looked over to see Calvin and Cassandra near the King and Queen's special podium, and then the dawning fury on the King's face as he saw them. Donald saw the anger in King Frederick's face and the horror that was painted on Calvin and Cassandra's.

"Stop! Run! Get out!" Donald yelled, but his voice was lost in the cheers as Grace brought her sword up. Drake didn't move fast enough and Grace was able to knock the sword from him. The applause was thunderous from everywhere, except those by the King. Grace smiled under the helmet and looked around, but when she looked up toward the King, her smile vanished.

"Impostor!" the King yelled at Grace, and the crowd fell silent. "You have stolen Sir Calvin's armor and fought under his identity! This is an offense that calls for your execution!"

Guards grabbed Donald from behind and dragged him forward. More guards dragged Grace forward and forced them in front of the King and Queen and the rest of the court. The two were forced down to their knees. Donald looked at Calvin, who forced his face into one of anger, furrowing his brows and gnashing his teeth, but fear was in his eyes.

"How dare you?" Calvin snapped.

Grace looked out from her helmet and knew her cousin was not really angry. He had probably already guessed who was in the sword ring in his stead. A great hush fell over the crowd. She looked around the faces and saw that many were waiting in shocked awe. Her eyes fell on Tristan, who looked annoyed and full of scorn.

"This is a great crime, impersonating a knight of the King," Frederick bellowed; his face red with anger. He fought to keep his voice level but was losing the battle. "Remove his helmet! I wish to see who would have the nerve to destroy years of tradition and break our code of chivalry."

Grace felt someone wrench the helmet from her head and once her hair tumbled down, not a word was spoken. The very air seemed to have been sucked from her lungs. From the onset she knew putting on the armor and being caught meant death, but she never believed anyone would actually learn the truth. Grace dared to look up. Tristan's face was bright red, Henry looked utterly confused, Calvin and Cassandra had matching expressions of utter horror, and the King was angriest of all.

"A woman," he whispered. His anger robbed him of his voice. "A woman?" he said, this time louder. "A woman!" he finally screamed. "A woman parading around as a man? And a nobleman, at that! Who taught you how courtly ladies should act? Women are not permitted to hold titles, and yet here one wears the armor of a knight! And this boy! This young man who pledged his service to Sir Calvin – he aids her willingly. Have these two forgotten their places? This affair reeks of witchcraft! Hang her immediately, for impersonating a knight and practicing witchcraft. Hang the manservant too, for aiding her in this mischief."

"Witchcraft?" Calvin said; looking at the King.

"How else could a woman beat a knight so well trained as Drake? Clearly she put a spell on him to ensure her victory. She must be killed for these heinous crimes."

"Your Majesty," Calvin broke in again. "Grace is my family, my only cousin, and though I am filled with a great anger toward her over this, there is still a family bond. We are of the same blood, the same proud lineage. Please, she must be punished, but can you not banish her? Banish her and my manservant, or force them into religious service?" Calvin looked pained just saying it. Grace lowered her eyes; this was not going to end well.

"You want to save the woman who made a mockery of your house in Arganis? Who disgraced herself and your fine stock? And to think the temples would want such heretics?" Calvin nodded. Frederick was as annoyed as he was angry. "The offended knight shows his mercy and I must respect that. If another will speak for this witch and the boy, then I shall see to it that they stand trial for heresy. Then shall justice be dispensed to your liking, Sir Calvin?"

Calvin bit his lip. If the King was convinced Grace was guilty of practicing witchcraft, then how could a court be persuaded otherwise? However, agreeing would allow time for him to perhaps protect her. He nodded and said, "That would be both wise and merciful of you, your Majesty."

"Then let someone else speak for this witch and her aid's trial."

No one spoke. Tears welled in Grace's eyes. Not a soul in the whole court would speak for either one. "Hang her!" Grace looked up and saw the voice belonged to Tristan. "She mocks us with her very presence. She has come into this court and bewitched us all, and now she must meet the hangman's noose."

Grace saw so much hate in his eyes. How could this be? He tried to win her over earlier, and now she was lower than dirt to him.

"I will speak for the girl," Henry said. "A witch may change her ways when given a second chance. Let them both stand trial and receive a fair hearing."

"I will speak for her as well." Everyone was surprised when Drake spoke up. He removed his helmet and handed it over to his squire. People murmured, unsure why their prince spoke for a woman who had just bested him in the sword ring. He walked forward to stand before his father. "I agree with Sir Henry. A wrongdoer may change her ways when mercy is shown."

"Very well," Frederick growled. He waved his hand to the guards. "Take her and the manservant to the pillory. Let them spend the night locked there, and in the morning we will let justice be dealt. Strip away that armor while you are taking them away. She mocks us by wearing it. I have been merciful this day, witch," Frederick said dismissively.

Grace lifted her head and locked eyes with Frederick; seeing his eyes filled with a fiery rage as he glared down at her. Grace's eyes narrowed as the guards grabbed her and Donald and pulled them away toward the pillory. She hated the King in that moment and wished to go for his eyes with her nails.

~*~*~

Grace's hands were locked up in the stocks. The heavy oak bar lay across her neck and her back cramped at the uncomfortable position she was in. The rest of the day passed with an amount of misery she once reserved for matters that involved her father. Humiliated, stripped of her inheritance and charged as a witch, certainly this was not what Leon and George wanted for her when they insisted she go to the tournament.

That entire afternoon, people came to stare at the unfortunate duo. Some just came out of curiosity, while others came to insult and throw things at the "witch." The reek of moldy cabbage and rotten tomatoes wafted up to Grace's nostrils. She and Donald each received their fair share of dirt and food thrown at them.

Losing all claims to her former life did not bother her as much as Tristan's reaction. He followed them to the stable and slapped Grace after she removed the armor. It stung not only because it hit her bruises, but also because he had tried to win her affection so soon before. He called her a witch and spat at her feet, saying she mocked everything sacred about the tournament by daring to compete. Then he claimed his feelings for her had been one of her spells. The final injury came when he said he would kill her himself if they ever met again. Then there was the guilt over Donald. He was not a bad man. A friend, a loyal servant, and yet now his honor was reduced to filth like hers. He hadn't said a word since they were taken away. Now night surrounded him, and the young man who was helpless in the pillory was humming.

The tune was one favored by fishermen in Arganis. The song told the tale of a beautiful maiden who became lost among the waves of the sea, waiting for her love to return. She cast herself down to the waves when she believed he'd never come home. Eventually he did, and upon hearing of her demise, he took to wandering the forests and letting his spirit inhabit the trees.

"The Lady Vivaine and her man, Joshua, despaired," Donald said upon finishing his tune. "That's why they both died as they did."

The light surrounding them was weak, but Grace thought she could make out tear stains on Donald's cheek, though it may have been a trick from the nearby torchlight. She knew her own face was soaked with salty tears. They mingled with the dirt, causing her to look sticky and dirty. Luckily no one would see her as she was now.

"Oh, Donald, what have I done to us?" Her voice broke at the end as a new wave of tears overtook her. "Even if we live, we will never be allowed to return to decent places." Grace halted in her despair, too overcome to continue vocalizing her grief.

"No doubt word is moving fast to all areas of Cesernan about this. But Sir Leon will never see his only niece cast out in the world, and Lord George never need know you returned to Arganis. We'll survive the trial and go straight back to your uncles." Donald's voice cracked just as Grace's had. His tears destroyed any hope Grace had of being comforted by his idea.

King Frederick had already marked them as guilty, and no

one could hope to survive that. "We'll return to Arganis, you'll see," Donald said again, softer this time.

Silence grew again between them, and other sounds of the night could be heard. The guards that stood within earshot were playing some sort of card game, a baby was crying in one of the houses that overlooked the city center, cats meowed, and rodents rustled through the trash heaps.

"I wish to see the witch," a familiar voice commanded.

"But, we've orders..." one of the guards said. Grace heard him quickly get to his feet. There was an uneasiness in his voice and movements.

"I am your prince and I command you let me see her and her manservant, *now*."

There was no further argument as Prince Drake was allowed to get closer to Grace and Donald. The guards were posted so that no one harassed or helped the two in the night. Now they flanked the Prince; each looking nervously at one another. Their orders were from Frederick, but Drake was his son. So now they wondered if they were doing right by allowing this.

"Unlock them. I wish to be able to look at them as decent people, not criminals."

"Now, Your Royal Highness, we can't be—"

"Sir! I have spoken. Do not refute me again." Drake's jaw was set and his eyes flashed an anger Grace didn't know he was capable of. This stern young man was not the same one she danced with earlier.

Shuffling awkwardly, one of the guards produced the keys and unlocked the stocks that held Grace. Then he moved on to Donald's. Grace stumbled. The heavy wood left her hands and ankles sore, while her back ached from being bent in the same position for so long. She knew she could not stand to perform the proper curtsey for Drake, so she threw herself on her hands and knees before his feet. Once freed, Donald did the same.

"You two..." Talking to the guards, the Prince produced a small leather pouch. "Go into the nearest tavern for a bit. I have private words to speak with these two."

"What if she should try to bewitch you?" the one who protested so much spoke.

"It is a chance I must take." He pushed the money into the man's hands. "Be gone with you." Without another word of argument, they were gone.

"Your Royal Highness," Grace pleaded. "Take pity on Donald. It was my scheming and not his. I will throw myself upon your father's mercy, but spare this man his life!"

At first there was no movement from the Prince. Daring to see what face he made, Grace looked up to see an odd expression plastered on his face. It wasn't hate, anger or even confusion. No, those were faces that were easily read. The Prince looked at her with something that was entirely new to her. He said nothing, and again she bowed her head. Drake's next move was more surprising than his visit.

He laughed and then took hold of Grace under the armpits before hoisting her onto her feet. Still too weak to move himself, Donald sat back on his ankles to see what was happening. The Prince held Grace awkwardly; his hands firmly on her upper arms, holding them to her sides. He kept her at arm's length and Grace felt him give her biceps a good, hard squeeze.

"Who taught you how to handle a sword? Some farmers teach their daughters in case they fear attack, but I have not yet heard of a noblewoman in this country taking up arms as a hobby. Perhaps in times of war, but..."

"Then you don't think Grace is a witch?" Donald said. He struggled to his feet. He now stood next to his friend, who was too stunned even to speak.

"I have heard old wives' tales about witches spelling whole courts, but I have never heard one where the witch allowed herself to get caught so easily. Nay – this girl is no witch in my eyes. But I can tell she has some training; enough that she knows how to take advantage of a tired knight and embarrass him before his country. So I ask you again, who taught you?"

"My—" she whispered before clearing her throat, "my Uncle Leon is the arms master in Arganis. Please forgive how I embarrassed you before everyone. Again I throw myself on your mercy."

"Enough people agree you are a witch, so my reputation is only slightly tarnished by this. Though rumors of your uncle's prowess with weapons have proved true if you could best me."

"You have competed for days and had matches that morning. Skill had no bearing in our match. I was simply lucky."

"If luck it was, it seems to have deserted you now. My father is set to see you both in the hangman's noose, and that's if he is merciful. Impersonating a knight, stealing his armor, embarrassing the heir…these are offenses not to be tolerated. But as I see it, you have merely been foolish and have done no real harm to anyone. As I said, enough think you are dabbling in the black arts, so I am no less a man to them."

Grace hung her head, knowing now for sure her death was hours away. Drake shook her gently until she looked into his eyes again.

"I will not see you two die. Your stupidity in the matter is not a crime. I cannot restore you to your old life, but I can offer freedom. I have some clothes that should disguise you. Leave tomorrow when the gates of Ursana open, and you can sneak out as the hordes of people try to enter."

"We cannot repay this kindness," Donald said.

"There is no need." Drake waved his hand dismissively. "However, you should realize that revealing your name and your home will put you in danger. I must ask you to promise not to speak of this to anyone. Bury your ancestry. That shall be your punishment. You are homeless and nameless now."

"Why help us, Drake?" Grace no longer feared him as the heir of the King. She was more afraid that he was not being sincere when he said they owed him nothing in exchange for his aid in their darkest hour.

"I want to be a merciful king, though not a weak one. Killing innocent folk such as you is not something I wish to live with. Exile is enough of a price to pay. It may well be harder on you than any of us now realize. But go now with my blessing for a safe journey, and do not embarrass young men further with your sword play, Grace."

As promised, Drake provided Grace and Donald with beggar disguises to get them out of the city. He found them a room to stay in and then left them to make their way.

~*~*~

While Drake freed Grace, the King was making his way through the guest wing. Frederick hated the idea that there were treacherous snakes in his midst. The witch of the Hilren line was gone, but her chief defender still remained. The King actively sought Henry of Egona after that night's feast. He knew the old knight would be pouring over his precious books.

Frederick entered Henry's chambers without so much as a knock, yet Henry was on his feet and bowing in seconds. "Majesty, I apologize for the condition of my chambers. I was not expecting company."

Frederick waved a hand, indicating Henry should sit again. He sat in an extra armchair Henry had. "Your defense of the witch was..." he paused, "...interesting. I recall a similar scandal some years back when you defended another who should have had his head on the chopping block."

Henry could tell Frederick was probing him for ill intentions; testing Henry's loyalties. He had done so on a regular basis for a number of years. "Meaning no disrespect, Majesty, but even your own son spoke up on that occasion when young Jonathon Mullery was on trial. And now he has spoken for the Hilren girl."

"Are you suggesting my son is filled with treachery?"

"Never. I am suggesting that perhaps your son and I share a different form of compassion than you do. It does not mean we undermine you." Henry watched the King's face carefully. Frederick was not convinced of Henry's loyalty, but by putting Drake – the only heir – into question, it caused Frederick to back down for the moment.

"You speak boldly, Henry."

"I am too old to do anything else boldly." This, luckily for Henry, caused Frederick to smile.

"Do not be too bold, though," Frederick said, and rose.

"Are you familiar with King William of Sera?" Henry asked, and Frederick paused to stare at him. "He ruled with an iron fist and showed mercy only when there was a direct benefit for himself. His ruthless rule caused heartbreak for many families, especially among the already dissatisfied peasants and their lords. Frustrated and angry, they saw fit to remove their king's head from his shoulders. It was twenty-five years before his grandson took the throne, after a very long and bloody civil war I might add, and only after he agreed to sign a contract saying the royal houses of Sera would understand and show mercy. This was to ensure times such as had been endured would not plague them again. That is why Sera has since adopted their attitude of peace and neutrality."

"What is it you are hinting at, Henry?"

"I have been reading up on Sera's history of late. You know I have made it a study of mine to understand our neighbors as best I can. I was just reading about William when you came in, and I only wished to share, Highness. Though I cannot help but worry about you."

"Speak plainly, Henry."

"Your 'compassion' to young Grace may cause more problems than you intend. Promising a fair trial may only incite trouble. You should send her to become a priestess for Kamaria. If she is allowed to go free, there is no telling where she will head or what lies she will spread about you and this court. In the temple to the moon goddess, at least you can keep an eye on her. If she dies, there are those who will question your mercy."

"You speak as though she'll have power wherever she goes, in death *or* life."

"Even the poorest peasants have voices. Commoners have been known to stir up the rabble," Henry said. He wanted to see to it that Grace was safe and remained so. If she was forced into the service of the goddess, she would be out of harm's way. With any luck, the story of King William and reminders of peasant revolts would sway Frederick.

"She has no voice. A disgraced noblewoman? Come now, who will heed her words? The only commoner capable of that is The Death Dealer, and I doubt he'd cross me. Go back to your books, Henry. Justice has been served this day."

Frederick knew what Henry was about. He saw that the book he was reading was not a history of Sera, but a book of folklore out of Eurur. The King nodded politely and left; mulling over Henry's behavior. Although he wasn't afraid to stand and defend those who met with Frederick's wrath, he was too old to cause any real trouble. Frederick would leave the aging knight alone.

~*~*~

The next morning, before anyone else rose, Drake confessed his "sin" to Frederick. The King was enraged at his son and his disdain for the young man would eventually become legendary, but for the moment he knew he would have to save face. The guards the Prince bribed were sent away from Ursana to work in the Nareroc Islands as punishment.

To the public, Frederick insisted another witch from Grace's coven managed to free her. For now she was able to walk free, but he issued a warning that should Grace be hidden in the city, if she dared to come near or corrupt the court again, she'd be killed. At Drake's behest, he did not send men out to seek her and bring her to justice. When all was said and done, Frederick determined to keep a close watch on his son and Henry of Egona, whom he believed was a willing accomplice in the mess.

~*~*~

The sun was setting as Grace and Donald trudged along the path. They had nothing – no food, no money, no extra clothing; just the beggar disguises from Drake. Grace at least still wore some of the extra clothing she'd had on under the armor, and Donald wore a grungy old tunic and tattered pants full of holes. He, with great reluctance, gave up the tunic he wore that proudly bore the crest and colors of Arganis. They were both hungry and tired, but the two vagabonds were trying to put as much distance between the castle and themselves as possible.

The young woman angrily kicked a stone that was in her

62

path. Donald was lost in his own thoughts. They couldn't even speak to one another. They both knew they were careless and stupid, especially since the Prince had been gracious enough to point that out. If they'd kept Calvin in his room, Grace might have succeeded. Or if they hadn't even tried to compete, all would have been right.

Behind them the noise of hoof beats arose, traveling fast. Grace looked at Donald and the two moved to the side of the road. No longer could they share the road with any members of nobility. The two lowered their heads and waited for the horses to pass.

They grew closer and closer and slowed as they came within a few feet of the travelers. Grace just wanted them to hurry along, but the horses stopped.

"Do not lower your eyes to us," Calvin's soft voice floated to Grace's ears.

She looked up and saw her cousin with Cassandra. He slid from his horse and pulled Grace into a hug. His right arm was wrapped up, so he wasn't able to give Grace the hug he wanted to. "I am so sorry, Grace. I could not let them kill you, but I never thought to break you free. Drake left me a note after Frederick announced another witch had freed you. We left straight away so we could see you one last time."

"No, I should be the one apologizing. I should not have been so rash, but I did not want to see Arganis have to forfeit the tournament. Forgive me, Calvin."

"Grace, do not worry about that. The tournament does not matter." Calvin released Grace and motioned to Cassandra. The maid got off her horse and pulled down two bags with her.

"My lady," she said; hugging Grace. She released her and then hugged Donald. "Sweet Donald."

"I thought you might need these things on the road ahead. You can use them to travel back home, or if you decide to break away, these supplies will serve you well. As long as I dwell in Arganis you are welcome – you know that, right?" Grace nodded. "Please write me from wherever you find yourself. I will worry too much if you and Donald fall out of touch." Calvin hugged Grace one last time and then mounted his horse again. "And this is for you – Henry of Egona wrote it. Be careful and do not keep us in the dark about your whereabouts."

Cassandra handed Donald and Grace their bags. "Watch over her, Donald, and do take care of yourselves." Cassandra hugged them both one last time and then mounted her horse.

After they were out of sight, Grace opened her bag. Two plain linen dresses, a small brown pouch of coin, and some food. She rummaged around some more and saw the glint of steel. Her sword and The Death Dealer clothes were stuffed into the very bottom.

She looked at Donald. It was apparent that Calvin and Cassandra hoped she would continue her work. She wondered what Donald thought, but then Donald guessed what was in Grace's bag and smiled. "I hear the port city of Glenbard is a breeding place for murderers and robbers. Perhaps we should head there."

Five

Glenbard was located on the eastern coast of Cesernan in Ursana, close to the northern border of Egona. Originally the city was meant to be the capital, and a small castle was built there. However, in the early days of Cesernan, pirates ravaged the shoreline and the capital was moved farther inland.

It took Grace and Donald three days in the blistering heat to arrive in the port city. The trip took so long because when the noonday sun was at its height, the two would stop and resume walking some hours later once the worst of the heat passed. By the time they finally made it, both were so sunburned they looked like tomatoes. Grace had every intention of getting a room at the local inn and staying inside for a week.

Glenbard was a sprawling city; twice as big as the city surrounding the King's castle. It was home to the largest port in Cesernan where scores of ships – military and merchant – passed every day. Its temple district sported the biggest and finest temples, even finer than the King's. Its merchant district had houses of the biggest, most fashionable, and latest designs from around the world. The marketplace filled every day with hundreds of vendors and shoppers. These vendors sold their wares in the large, open market space in the center of the city, while nearby prostitutes sold theirs from doorways and alleys. Wherever they went, children were under-foot. Some playing, some pick pocketing, and others begging for a meal.

Upon entering the city, travelers were assaulted with a host of smells. Some were pleasant, such as fresh bread and exotic fruits; others curdled the stomach, like the latrines or horse droppings yet to be shoveled from the street. The colors flying about the city were no less potent. Colorful signs hung from doorways to indicate the trade that was to be found inside. Vandals took to some buildings more than others; decorating doors and walls with colorful displays against the King or in favor of a certain woman.

Together, the two outcasts made their way through the city's narrow streets. Donald stopped in front of a tavern that appeared to have rooms on the upper level. "I suppose this is as good a place as any. We are not likely to find the best or safest lodgings here in Glenbard." So far though, the area where this tavern and inn were housed looked safer and more pleasant than any other they had passed.

"The Angel Tavern." Grace looked at the old wooden sign hanging outside, quite worn from weather and time. The picture of an angel was cracked and faded, but one could tell the angel was once very beautiful when her paint was still fresh. "Let's go get ourselves a room, then."

Donald held the door open for Grace and she stepped lightly into the common room. It was only midday, but the tavern was already bustling. Most of the fisherman and merchants of Glenbard were escaping the noon heat by taking their meal in the common room. The place stank of sweat, ale, and the faint smell of vomit. The heat always brought up smells that had long since been dead.

Grace looked around and tried to get a feel for the inn, and sensed no real danger for her or Donald. The people within did not seem to care that two strangers entered. A few looked up, but only for a quick glance at the newcomers. Grace liked this place. She liked the idea that people might not care what she looked like or where she came from.

Donald took her by the elbow and led her to the innkeeper's desk. "Excuse me, sir?"

A burly man with a balding head and scraggly gray beard looked at Donald. He was probably a strong man in his youth, but years in an inn had taken their toll on him. More specifically, in his expanding belly. "Yes?"

"Are you the innkeeper here?"

"I am, and who might you be, laddy?"

"I am Donald and this is my friend, Grace. We are looking for two rooms to rent."

"Well you've come to the right place. There are plenty of rooms here…that is, if you've got the means to rent them."

Grace turned away as Donald and the innkeeper haggled over

a room price and continued her scan of the inn. A group of people stood near the stairs. They seemed to be standing around an older, fierce-looking man who was seated, drinking from a pint and smoking a pipe. He had dark hair peppered with gray, a trimmed beard, and his dark eyes took in the whole room. Every now and again he waved his hand and one of his followers rushed off. A teenage girl with curly blonde hair sat on his right side. She had an intense look about her and looked as fierce as her male counterpart. Grace watched them for a minute before moving her eyes elsewhere.

Finally, her eyes landed on a lone figure seated in a dark corner. His head was bent toward his food and drink, and he looked very sullen and angry. He sported short brown hair and a trimmed goatee, and was attired in black breeches and a gray shirt. He was the only person in the entire inn not conversing with anyone. As though he sensed staring eyes, he looked up and caught Grace's gaze; each holding their stare. Normally others looked away under Grace's watchful eyes, but this man just kept staring.

They probably would have stared at each other until day ended, but Donald touched Grace's arm and she was forced to look away.

"We have two rooms. Let's go unpack, Grace."

Calvin had given the two plenty of money to live on until they could get everything sorted out. Donald planned on unpacking and going to see what kind of work could be had around the port. His father was a carpenter in Arganis, so he hoped a carpenter in Glenbard had need of an apprentice. Their small store of gold should be able to buy an apprenticeship.

Grace planned on unpacking and then going to talk to the innkeeper about being a barmaid for the inn. If that failed, she wasn't sure what other jobs she could do that would keep her tattered dignity intact. She wasn't even sure she could pass as a barmaid.

~*~*~

Donald left and Grace found her way back into the common

room. She strode up to the innkeeper's desk and coughed politely to get his attention.

"Can I help you, miss?"

"Yes, sir. I am in need of work and thought you may be in need of an extra hand around here, perhaps a barmaid? I would be grateful and indebted to you if you would but give me the chance."

"You're awfully well spoken, aren't you? Not really the way my serving wenches usually are. They've all put sailors to shame with their harsh words. But I haven't the use for another wench, in any case. The ones I have are sass-mouthed women who aren't worth what I pay them. I don't need another one hanging around, even if she can fool us all with soft words."

"You have no jobs I could do for you? None at all? I promise I am not a sass mouth."

"I need another stable hand. You look too prim to be mucking out my stables, though."

"I can take care of horses for you. Horses, cows, any kind of animal. And I learn fast; I can muck out the stalls." Grace had never mucked out a stall in her life, but the thought of going into Glenbard looking for work was terrifying. Grace didn't know how a woman could earn a living without selling herself, and she was not interested in such a move.

The innkeeper looked Grace over. To his eyes she looked small and rather helpless, but he liked her determination and the fact she didn't mind getting dirty for the job. Still, the Angel had only ever taken on sturdy young men to aid in the stables, not small, frail girls. "You'd have to start every day at sunrise and work until sunset. At sundown, Liam comes in to take care of the animals. You'll be working with Mayhew, who likes everything done nice and fast and has no patience for anyone. He'll work you to the bone and it'll make no difference to him that you're a girl. Think you can handle that? Plenty of durable men haven't been able to."

"Yes sir, I can keep up and handle the stables."

The innkeeper held out his hand to her. "Name's Jim Little."

"Grace."

"Be up bright and early tomorrow for your first day." Jim smiled down at Grace. "You look plucky. Mayhew may have a hard time driving you away." The innkeeper smirked but didn't share any more of his thoughts, and she had the feeling she was being made the butt of a joke.

Grace was still quite pleased with herself, even though she knew it wasn't going to be easy. All she knew about taking care of horses was how to groom, saddle and unsaddle one. She would manage, though. She would just have to keep reminding herself that she'd have more freedom here than she ever had at court.

"Working for old Mayhew, are you?" Grace looked up and saw the teenage girl she noticed earlier. Now that she was closer, she didn't look as fierce as she had at a distance. "He can be quite a pain. Hates everyone, except of course, those blasted animals." She extended her hand to Grace. "Hi, I'm Ridley Hunewn."

Grace gladly accepted her hand. "Grace." Again, she neglected to give her family name. Surely some bit of news had already been received in Glenbard about the shameful woman who tried to compete.

"And new to Glenbard, I see. I noticed you and that man enter a while back. We always like to see strangers around here because they bring the best news. I love news from outside Glenbard and Ursana. That's why I love tournament season; many of our merchants head to the castle area to set up shop, and they bring back the greatest stories of the tournament. I don't suppose you have any stories from the tournament?"

The girl clearly liked to talk, but she was friendly and didn't seem to judge Grace as harshly as the women of the court had. Though at first glance she looked fierce and uninviting, now that she was actually talking to Grace she found all that sternness melted away. This girl clearly never had any real reason to be angry with anyone. "I actually come from Arganis, but I spent a few days at the tournament. What I saw was exciting."

"Arganis?" Ridley began; leading Grace toward an empty table. "We rarely get someone from so far north here. Only a few from there ever pass through, and most never stay to tell us about it. Or if they do, it's always about the lumber business up north. How boring! They say that's where The Death Dealer is from." Ridley's eyes brightened as she said it. "Have you ever seen him?" Ridley sat down at a corner table and Grace sat across from her.

"Only once, just outside my village."

"Was he as wonderful and courageous as the tales tell?"

"I did not get the chance to really speak to him. He was walking a young woman home after she was attacked in the woods. He rescued her. He seemed quite dashing and heroic from what the woman said." Grace felt guilty lying to her new-found friend, but The Death Dealer was not a secret easily laid out on the table. Even if it was, she didn't want to let anyone in on it.

Ridley sighed and got a wishful look in her eye. "I do hope one day I will get the chance to meet him. Glenbard needs someone like him hanging around. The king's guards do nothing but bully us lower classes. They expect bribes or else no aid will be provided. How's an honest person supposed to raise money for protection?"

"That's awfully funny coming from the Princess of Thieves," the man Grace noticed before spoke from his corner.

"Princess of Thieves?" Grace turned back to Ridley.

"Around here we're known as the 'Fisherman's Collective', but most people call us the 'Thieves Guild'; knowing full well none of us fish. Don't look so shocked. People need to scrape a living around here. We don't steal from our own class—often— not now that Marcus is in charge. We try to only steal from those who can afford it. We have honor, you know," she snapped back at the corner dweller. "And we don't attack folk in dark alleys, and we most certainly don't kill defenseless people."

"*You* do not do those things, but there are those in your precious Thieves Guild that see to such deeds. And you steal and pick fights with rogue thieves. If your precious Death Dealer ever came to Glenbard, I bet he starts by cleaning out the Guild," the man continued.

"He would not! He only goes after bullies, and there is no one in the Guild who's a bully."

"You live with rather strange delusions, Ridley. First you tell her the guards only bully the lower classes, when you know full well they usually only bully your kind. Now you tell her there are no bullies in the Guild? Ha! You forget that even Marcus took the Guild's crown through murder and treachery." The man's rant complete, he looked down into his mug.

Ridley turned away from the man in the corner and crossed her arms over her chest. She huffed loudly and angrily and took a few deep breaths. "It's best if you stay away from Jack Anders. He's just an old grump who tries to drag everyone down into his rut."

"I'm not old," he said. Ridley ignored him.

"Used to be a rusher at the Emerald Rose." Grace shook her head, indicating she had no idea what that was. "Sorry, lass…the Rose is on the port side and is the most dangerous place in Glenbard. Murders are regular there and rushers don't usually last more than a week, but old Jack lasted a year; breaking skulls, fingers and making troublemakers disappear. The experience has left him less than happy."

Grace looked over at Jack. He did not look to be much older than his mid-twenties. He did look a bit angry and his face was lined with cares, but underneath it all Grace saw a bit of decency. She wondered what made him so bitter. She looked away from Jack and back to Ridley.

"What is the Thieves Guild, exactly?"

"Oh, we're a group of 'scoundrels' as the guards call us, who banded together for safety. Vandals, thieves, people down on our luck, that's where we all come from. We give to our families and friends who need it. The city magistrates and guard captains have tried to root us out for years, but we're clever. We can all sneak around and get into places most other people can't. People judge us harshly because we're comprised of thieves, but we don't hurt other people unless they hurt us first." She lowered her voice. "Jack is right about some of our ranks being just as bad as murderers, but we root them out best we can." Ridley must have noticed the shocked look on Grace's face and laughed. "Don't judge us too severely. We're not bad people, and old Marcus is our king. He makes sure we follow a code of honor around here." Ridley motioned to the fierce-looking man Grace saw when she first entered.

"And you don't mind that your father does this?"

"Don't be fooled by the title 'Princess of Thieves'. It's no more than a term of endearment from some of the men."

"Marcus is not your father, then?"

"He is like my father. My own pa was in the Guild, and when my parents died I came into Marc's care. I've been in the Guild since I was six."

"How old are you now?"

"Sixteen, and I don't regret those early years as a pickpocket or these last years as a full and proper member of the Guild."

Grace smiled and nodded. She became The Death Dealer to punish those who preyed on the weak and poor. And it's true; she would have attacked the Guild outright if she had not learned all this information from Ridley. If the Guild moved with any force, she'd have seen her life in Glenbard end rather swiftly.

She had to take into account all that Anders said. If there were those in the Guild who needed punishing, she would see to them. Grace would see how the Guild worked before deciding if she should go against them as a whole, though. Until that time, she would go after those who attacked and tried to kill the weaker folk. It would be safer than taking on the thieves all together.

"Do you always give this information so freely?"

"You'll hear about the Fishermen's Collective often enough, and I'd hate for you to be provided with false information." She cut her eyes to Jack. "We're not really a secret, after all. And you'll be working here, so you need to know who your bedfellows are."

~*~*~

Ridley readily agreed to show Grace around the city when she asked for a guide. The young Princess of Thieves was ready to do whatever she could to make her new friend more comfortable in her new home. Grace was thankful she had someone to talk to aside from Donald.

Ridley took her by the dock and showed her all the ships that were coming into port. Grace knew many of the flags the ships flew under. There was the crowned sun of Eurur, the golden star of Archon, and the two rearing silver horses from Sera. A myriad of other countries were in the port; countries Grace was not even aware of. Ridley had her by the arm and guided her along, but Grace's eyes stayed on the port. She was in utter awe of how many came to Cesernan to trade. A sudden longing to sail out to sea overcame Grace. She sighed heavily as Ridley turned a corner and the view of the port was lost.

Grace's eyes widened as they entered the next area of Glenbard.

"This is the temple district," Ridley explained.

Grace did not need to be told where they stood. The first temple was the biggest of all three on the street, and Grace was familiar with it. The insignia of the sun on the huge iron doors gave it all away. This was the temple to Ciro. The roof was domed and made mostly from glass so the light could enter and shine on the altar. Many high pillars ran around the temple, all of them lined in gold. Several smaller houses were next to the temple, each one with a domed roof; these were the houses of the priests of Ciro.

Across the street was an equally large temple with the sigil of a crescent moon on its iron doors. The temple to Kamaria. The roof here was high arched, but huge windows opened in the east and in the west. It was for when the moon rose and set, and it was built that way to allow the moon's light to shine on the altar. It even sported a bell tower. This temple had the same type of pillars as Ciro's did, only they were lined with silver; Kamaria's color. Smaller houses were next to it, which housed the priestesses of Kamaria. Leading away from Ciro and Kamaria's temples was a road to three, moderately-sized stone buildings.

"That serves as a dormitory for priest and priestess trainees.

They get locked in there for a full year without contact with the rest of the city! Can you imagine?"

Grace confessed, "My uncle was afraid I would be unmarried forever and he wanted to send me here to serve the Divine Twins. I came to Glenbard to find a husband and avoid those enclosed grounds."

The third and final temple was entirely new to Grace. Every province had a temple to Ciro and Kamaria, but this third one was different. It was much smaller and plainer, and had the image of a winged star on the wooden doors. It sported a high vaulted ceiling and a few stained glass windows.

"Who is this temple for? I am not familiar with the sign on the door."

"Diggery, the goddess of protection and guardian of lost souls."

Diggery was not an unknown deity to those in Arganis, but she wasn't held in the same esteem as the Divine Twins. People in the north prayed to her to help guide them through hard times, but Grace had never seen or heard of a temple being erected in her honor.

"This temple is quite new to me. In Arganis, small figurines may be found of Diggery in wolf form, but no temples. Why has it been built here?"

"Glenbard is a refuge for the damned and outcast. Many here consider Diggery their patron, so why not build a temple to honor her?"

Grace looked at the winged star and knew where she would be coming after dinner this evening.

"Come on – there's still more to see." Ridley took Grace by the arm again and led her away from the temples.

~*~*~

"Stay here and I'll get us some dinner," Ridley said, and had Grace sit where they did earlier that day. The Angel Tavern was getting pretty full and Ridley wanted to make sure they had a place to sit and eat their dinner.

All around the tavern, people were looking at her; whispering and snickering. Most were big, burly men who seemed to think there was something amusing about her, but Grace was unable to put her finger on the exact reason. She turned her head from side to side and tried to count just how many people were eyeing her.

A man's voice said from behind her, "The men have a bet going with Jim Little. You see, you were only hired as a joke to help Mayhew muck out stables." Grace turned to face Jack Anders and noted that he hadn't moved from his secluded corner.

"Do you ever move from that spot, sir?"

"Of course, but only when the tavern is ablaze." He looked at all those looking upon Grace. "Now there," he continued, seeing Grace scowl, "don't let the bet hurt your precious feelings. This sort of thing happens whenever someone new is brought in to deal with Mayhew. The only difference this time is that you are a female. Most women around here are too smart to work for him."

Grace turned away and caught sight of Ridley across the tavern. She waved excitedly to Grace.

"Now that she's found you, you'll never get her to shut up."

Grace snapped her attention back to Jack. "If being rude and bitter is your choice then fine, but you shouldn't try to bring the rest of us down into your rut. Ridley is a sweet girl and has been kind enough to show me around. What reason do I have to want her to be quiet?"

"I'm just telling you – once she starts, she won't stop." Jack took a puff from his pipe. "I find it all very funny that someone as proper as you is becoming friends with someone as low as Ridley." Grace gave Jack a nasty glare. "Ridley's a nice kid, but you two aren't exactly from the same game."

"What are you talking about?"

Jack looked around and got out of his chair. He leaned over the table and hung his face in Grace's. "I'm no fool. I was once a stable hand for the King, and I saw all the knights. You don't have to play this game with me, Grace. You're from Arganis; your accent proves it to any who would doubt. But you have Lady Dedre's nose and you have Lord Daniel's eyes: little gray orbs of malice, and his deceptively tiny ears that no doubt catch all rumors to use for blackmail. Whatever you did to get out of court must have been very daring or very stupid."

Grace wanted to respond, but her voice was stuck in her throat as Jack's green eyes bore down on her. She wished she could speak, yell, or simply throw things in his direction. She did none of those things; she just continued to glare at him.

"Jack! Leave poor Grace alone!" Ridley's voice cut through their tense stare-down. Jack backed away from the table and returned to his own seat.

"I was just having a chat with your new friend."

"She doesn't want to chat with you," Ridley snapped. She placed a plate of potatoes and fish down in front of Grace. "It's the cook's specialty. It's actually all he can make that doesn't taste rotten."

Grace forced a smile and dug into her plate. Ridley chatted on and on, but Grace didn't hear any of it. Her eyes kept straying toward Jack, who openly watched her with interest.

"Don't be bothered by him," Ridley finally said. "He likes to ruffle feathers. He's really quite harmless."

Grace pushed her plate away. "I'm sorry, I have lost my appetite. I am going for a walk."

Ridley nodded and Grace rose from her seat. "You scared her away!" she heard Ridley say when she was some feet away.

~*~*~

Diggery's temple was deserted, so Grace sat near the altar with her head bowed. She certainly needed guidance, especially after her encounter with Jack. How was it possible for one person to get so far under her skin? She had never before been so irritated by a person so quickly. He said her eyes were filled with malice...no, filled with malice just like her father's. And ears that caught rumors for blackmail? What was *that* supposed to mean? Anders stood there and made dreadful assumptions about her father.

This sort of thing never would have happened back at court. Then again, the people at court would have been fake and sweet to her face while chatting behind her back. Did this mean Jack's honesty was a mixed blessing?

Grace began cursing her choices. Her choice to train like Calvin, her choice to enter the sword ring in his stead, her choice to come here. What did she do to her life?

Someone sneezed in the back of the temple and Grace lifted her head and looked around. A girl not much older than seventeen was in the back. She was quite tall, with straight black hair that fell well past her shoulders and flawless skin of a dusky hue. She wore black breeches and a long, black, buttoned-up riding jacket, though Grace saw a white shirt peeking out underneath. What really caught Grace's attention were her deep purple eyes. Grace had seen the same color at dusk, when the sun's light was chased out for the soft light of the moon and stars. And like the twilight purple of the sky, this young woman's eyes went on forever.

"I am very sorry to disturb your prayers. I am meeting someone here and it is rare to find others around during the evenings. And here I thought I would have the temple to myself."

Grace smiled and shook her head. "It's no trouble. I was going to leave soon."

The young woman walked up the aisle and slid in next to Grace. "Mind if I join you until you do? It's nice to have company while I wait."

"Please have a seat. It is always nice to meet someone new."

The woman smiled and looked toward the altar. Unlike the temples of Ciro and Kamaria, there were no statues of Diggery in human form. Grace had only ever seen Diggery depicted in animal form. Since her image was rare in Arganis, Grace always assumed her lack of human form was due to her lack of followers so far north. Diggery was always shown in the form of a great black wolf in Arganis and it seemed to be the same here. On the altar there was a statue of a prone black wolf. Someone had obviously been in recently and adorned it with a wreath of red roses. It seemed to make the wolf more approachable.

"It always makes me wonder why Diggery comes as a wolf," Grace finally said. "She picks an animal many fear and hate, yet she comes and comforts them."

The woman shrugged. "What the gods do is a mystery to mortals, I suppose." She turned to Grace and held out her hand. "My name is Kit."

"Grace."

"Are you new to Glenbard?"

"I just arrived this morning."

"Ah, it is not as bad as many elsewhere say. I've heard the word *uncivilized* thrown around a lot, or *cesspool*. Glenbard is as clean as any other port city, but its reputation remains. I visit here every few years, and out of the other port cities I enter, this one is one of the nicer ones. The Fishermen's Collective keeps murders down because they cannot stand people killing their workers or their families. It was not always so, but these days Marcus sees to it. Other cities have just let the murderers take control until honest, hard-working people refuse to live there."

"Have you traveled much? You don't look old enough to have seen the world yet."

"My father is a sailor. I used to go harbor to harbor with him, but now I travel about on my own. The wandering life can be good, though I must admit it is not for everyone. It is full of danger and a great deal of uncertainty. I go weeks without knowing where my next meal shall come from. And the diseases men endure at sea! Descriptions of such are not suited to polite company. I always tell people to stay home if death, disease and blood worry them." Kit smiled.

Before the woman came in, Grace was praying for guidance on whether or not she should just sail from Cesernan altogether, but Kit's words shook her dream of sailing to the core. The very mention of blood and death brought her back to the dead man. His blood tried to drown her in dreams most nights, and she wasn't ready to see the bloated corpses of sailors. Without intending to, Kit gave Grace advice on her next move in Glenbard.

Someone cleared his throat in the back of the temple. Grace and Kit both turned and saw Jack Anders. "You came." Kit turned back to Grace and said, "Jack is an old family friend. You should stay and chat with us. I always make it a point to visit him when I am in Glenbard. Come join us, Jack."

"I should be going." Grace rose from her seat and brushed quickly past Jack. As she reached the door, she turned back to Kit. "A pleasure meeting you, miss. Maybe I will have a chance to see you before you wander on."

"I am sure we will. Good night, Grace."

~*~*~

Grace sat on Donald's bed as he paced the room. Donald underestimated the cost of an apprenticeship in Glenbard. If they were to survive their first few weeks in Glenbard, they couldn't afford the opportunity for Donald to apprentice with a carpenter or anyone else, for that matter. He heard of a few merchant ships sailing to the Nareroc Islands that were looking for able-bodied men. The islands were located between Cesernan and Sera and were famous for their spices. Both countries claimed various parts of the islands, and a great deal of trade took place there.

If Donald took a job on one of the ships, it would take him a week to sail to the islands, a week to help load and gather what was needed, and then a week to return home; weather permitting, of course. When Donald told her, Grace encouraged him to go, but the former manservant was hesitant.

"In Arganis we had Cassandra to protect you, but here you only have me. If you were to go out one night and get wounded with your...duty, and I was gone, who would help you? Who would take you to a healer?"

"I am capable of watching over myself. You should take a position on one of the merchant ships. The money will be good, and we can't live on what Calvin gave to us forever."

"They always have spots open for young men on those ships, so I have plenty of time to decide. I'd rather not go. I wouldn't be able to forgive myself if I left and something horrible happened to you. We are in a more dangerous area than Arganis."

"Donald, sleep on it." Grace reached out and took his elbow, and he stopped pacing for a moment. "We both know you should take it. Just think about it tonight. The answer will come to you, and I think you already know what it is."

Grace wished Donald a good night and returned to her room. She had planned to go out and watch the Thieves Guild, but decided it would not be in her best interest to ruin the bet on herself. There would be time for The Death Dealer in the weeks to come, but now was not it. She needed to learn Glenbard first so she could move easily when night fell.

~*~*~

"You shouldn't tell anyone what you know about that Grace girl, Jack. I saw her banishment when Frederick called for her hanging. Why cause the poor child any more stress?" Kit said as Jack rose from his seat in the temple. The two had spent the last two hours catching up on one another's lives. Mostly Jack spoke while Kit listened. Now at the end, he told her about Grace.

"She has done a brave thing," Kit said softly.

"A stupid thing, sounds like. Donning her cousin's armor? Where's the bravery in such a stupid act?"

"She did it knowing the consequences, and showed the court she was not just a breeder. Foolhardy, yes, but still brave. Don't punish her for that."

"She doesn't belong here, Kit," Jack protested. "She's probably just like all those other women in court; all the ones I knew when I still served under Frederick. Grace should just go to some small farming village, marry, and have babies. It was her path in life when she was still in Arganis. Why change it because she's not nobility anymore?"

"You do not know her path," Kit said. "And you most certainly should not drive her away from Glenbard."

"I can't think of a reason why I shouldn't."

Jack turned to leave. As usual, his visit with Kit ended with him in a foul mood. "I can think of a good reason." Jack stopped and waited for what she would say.

"She is not Danielle."

Jack turned around slowly and met Kit's gaze. "What did you say?"

"You think Grace is like Danielle. I can tell, even without you mentioning her name. It has been eight years, Jack. Not all ladies of the world are the same. And look at Grace – already she has proven she is a better person. She has not submitted to her grief like others who have fallen on the same bad luck. She could be your friend, Jack. Do not let your grief and hate consume you like so many before you. You would do well to learn from her."

Jack bowed his head and walked briskly out the temple door. Anger and confusion boiled beneath the surface. He wanted to burst through the doors at the Angel and scream Grace's secret to everyone inside, but he couldn't. As the tavern came into sight, something held him back.

"Damn," he muttered under his breath and continued to walk. He headed down to the docks, sat at the water's edge and watched the moon travel across the night sky.

Six

The world was still dark when Grace dressed in the clothes she took from Calvin. She quietly closed her door and tiptoed past Donald's room and down into the common room. Only Jim was up and about, getting things ready for the tavern's breakfast.

"Mornin', Grace," he said as she moved past his desk. "Let me take you out to meet Mayhew."

Grace followed Jim Little. It was impossible for her to read him, but she wanted to know on what side he fell in regards to the bet. Was he one of the folks saying she'd fail outright, or did he have faith? Did he hire her only for amusement's sake? Jim said nothing as he took her out to the stables and led her to an old, gray-haired man, starting to bend with age, who eyed Grace with suspicion. "I want a boy to work here!" he snapped at Jim. "This girl is too scrawny to do the work, and she'll fall in love with any male who boards a horse here."

"No one in Glenbard is going to work for you, so I had to hire a willing stranger," Jim snapped back. "Besides, young Grace here is a good solid worker; you can tell by the honesty in her face." He must have a wager that she'd last. Jim pushed Grace forward and she slowly extended her hand to Mayhew.

He looked at it as though she were diseased and pointed to a line of stalls, five on each side. "Start mucking those out until I tell you to stop or you finish!" He pushed a shovel and a pail into her hands. "Do it now!"

When mid-morning crept up on them, Grace had thoroughly cleaned three of the ten stalls. She would have done more, except Mayhew was never satisfied with her work and she continually went back to redo them.

Mayhew went off to enjoy a mid-morning meal and Grace grumbled as she entered the next stall. The horse in this stall was a proud looking gelding. Grace had never seen a horse so fine in all her years. It had a finely kept brown coat and looked at Grace with thoughtful brown eyes. As she entered his stall the gelding stepped toward her, nuzzled her breast and nipped her shirt;

hoping to find food.

She gently patted his muzzle and laughed. "Sorry, boy...I don't have anything for you." The horse didn't seem to understand and continued to inspect Grace's clothing for food. "Do you have a name, you sweet animal?"

"Pilgrim." Grace looked over the stall wall and saw Marcus, the man Ridley called the King of the Thieves Guild. This was the man Grace would need to watch the most in order to understand exactly how the Guild operated. Up close, like Ridley, he was softer. He smiled. Looking at him now, she wondered how such a kindly looking man could have become the King of Thieves through murder and treachery.

She wasn't sure how to address him so she bowed her head in respect. "Is he your horse, sir—er, Majesty?"

Marcus laughed at Grace's attempt to flatter him. "You can just call me Marcus, girl. The 'King of Thieves' title is just to scare off rogue thieves. And no, I wish I could claim Pilgrim as mine, but he's not. That horse belongs to Jack Anders."

Grace looked over the horse again. How could that be possible?

"Strange, I know. How can such a well mannered horse belong to someone as resentful as Jack? No one really knows. He used to be a stable hand for Frederick, and this horse must have been a parting gift."

"I wasn't just *any* stable hand; I was King Frederick's best stable hand at his castle in Ursana. And I was given that horse before he was weaned from his mother. No one expected Pilgrim to grow into the horse he is now, and many are kicking themselves for giving him up so willingly."

"Such a touching tale, Jack." Marcus clapped him on the back and laughed some more. "But it's still a marvel that horse didn't take on your demeanor. It's loving and kind; so unlike you."

"Don't think I didn't try to make him mean, Marcus."

Marcus laughed again. "Whatever you say, Jack," he said, and bowed his head to Grace. "Enjoy mucking out the rest of the stables here. Do a good job, and someday Mayhew may warm up to you. If not, replace the feathers in his pillow with some dung." With a wink and a smile, Marcus turned and left.

Grace glared at Jack when Marcus was out of sight. "What do you want?"

"I'm here to make sure nothing happens to my horse," he said as he grabbed a saddle and bridle. He clearly wanted to take the horse out for a ride. "What does a girl like you know about mucking out stalls?"

"You think you're so smart, Jack Anders. You think I am just some stupid girl who was disgraced; that I cannot take care of myself. But I will have you know I am capable of watching over myself. There are plenty who did care about me and they're still my friends, despite the fact I have been reduced to mucking out stables."

"Friends that care about you?" Jack laughed and it left Grace feeling cold and yet, at the same time, white hot with anger. "Friends, you say. Tell me then, a pretty thing like yourself – what boy, what friend in court loved you and then left you when you were exiled? What 'man' of the court allowed you to be reduced to this?" Grace's thoughts ran to Tristan and how he acted as she left in shame. Jack picked up on Grace's thoughts and feelings. "What did he say when you left? What cruel thing did he utter in your ear as you walked by, completely disgraced? What brave knight was he?"

Grace choked back tears as thoughts of Tristan's cruelty came back to mind. She hoped to be strong and forget him, but Jack's words coaxed it out of her.

"Sir Benjamin? No, he never showed affection, only received it. Sir Thomas? Nah, he never shows interest in young ladies. Perhaps Sir Tristan of Escion?" Grace clenched her jaw and balled her fists. "Yes, there it is. I knew him. He was like his father; arrogant and selfish. Though he charmed the women by putting on a sweet face. His reputation was not so innocent when it came to pretty faces." Jack walked into the stall and circled Grace; putting the saddle aside. "It doesn't surprise me you were in his sights, and it doesn't surprise me you returned the attraction. You're just like the rest. Tristan might have married you, but he would have cast you aside like his father threw his mother aside." Jack stepped closer. "After a few children, you would be no more to Tristan than one of his hunting dogs or his horses. But looking at you now, I suppose he already sees you as such."

Grace was speechless. She was absolutely stunned and unsure what to say in response to Jack.

"Jack!" The angry voice of Mayhew cut through and brought Grace from her trance. Her eyes turned into slits as she stared up at Jack. "That girl has stables to clean and saddles to polish! Leave her alone!"

Jack looked at Grace and waited for her to answer. She took a deep breath and steadied her voice. "You are a dog, Master Anders. I despise you and your cruelty. Refrain from speaking to me ever again!"

Jack shrugged his shoulders to indicate his lack of caring. However, his upper lip curled; suggesting to Grace he did care and was somewhat angered by this exchange. He led Pilgrim out; planning to saddle the horse outside the stable to avoid any more conversation with Grace.

~*~*~

"Enough lollygaggin', girl. Them horses ain't goin' to muck their own stalls!" Mayhew barked at her. Taking up the shovel again, Grace went back to work. Though now, not only was Mayhew breathing down her neck, Jack's words burned in her mind as well. She gritted her teeth and began to work harder.

What right did he have to make such assumptions? He had only been a lowly stable boy at the palace. But his words hit a chord, and that made Grace even angrier. Not just at Jack, but at Tristan too. As the thoughts slowly burned a hole through Grace's soul, she worked harder and faster, much to Mayhew's surprise. After a while, a young boy returned and led Pilgrim into his stall. Mayhew looked after the horse while continuing to watch Grace.

The old stable hand watched with interest. Something had lit a fire under her, and now the girl worked with one solid purpose. She ground her teeth, gripped the handle of her shovel with a new found fury, and she kept this pace when anyone else would have tired. Finally Mayhew decided to award her with a break. "Girl, enough for now. You'll be no good if ya exhaust yourself before lunch. Get something to eat."

Grace pushed the shovel into Mayhew's hands and stormed into the common room. Jack was in his usual corner, smoking a pipe and glowering at the world, but no one else was about. Instead of wasting her meal in the same vicinity as Jack, Grace headed into the kitchen.

Jim Little and the cook, Georges – a fat, old, bearded man – were talking over mugs of ale. Jim cocked an eyebrow. It was impressive to see that the girl made it so far, but no doubt she was finished now.

"Is there any chance for a meal? Mayhew expects me back." The full force of the morning was catching up with Grace. Her anger was running itself out, and that made her tired. Still, she had more work to do. She'd prove to everyone how strong and capable she was.

The cook and Jim exchanged looks. From where Grace stood, she couldn't tell if they were impressed or concerned. "Of course, lassie." Jim pulled a chair out and beckoned her to sit at the table with himself and the cook. "Master Georges will ladle ya out some soup. I'm sure you're in need of it after a morning with Mayhew." Georges ambled around the table to a giant pot that hung over the fire.

"He has said little of my performance since his return from lunch."

"He'll be unbearable when you return. Meals always put him in a more pleasant mood." Georges placed a bowl of unidentifiable broth and chunks before Grace and she ate it gratefully.

~*~*~

Grace's survival in the stables was the talk of the tavern later that night when she ate dinner with Ridley. She ignored it all and simply concentrated on the night ahead; keeping a close eye on Marcus's table while she ate. Memorizing faces and voices, she turned in for the night around ten and at midnight, took to the streets as The Death Dealer. She was much too tired to actually do much, but she went out to learn the city better.

Waiting in the shadows outside of the Angel, she trailed the first thief to exit. If what Ridley said was true, then this thief would take from a merchant or two and then bring the gold or silver back to Marcus. What happened after that was a mystery, because Ridley wouldn't offer any more hints as to what Marcus did with his spoils. Or what other activities his men were up to.

Grace wasn't sure what she hoped to see when she trailed the thief into the night. Part of her wanted to witness more than petty theft from a merchant's house. If the Thieves' Guild committed murder or anything else, she could go after them without worrying she would offend her new friend.

She felt wrong allying herself with Ridley, given the girl's profession, but Grace wanted Marcus to be as charitable as his adopted daughter claimed. Partly because she liked Ridley and found a friend in her, but also because she knew death would be waiting for her if she tried to take on the Guild.

Thus far, the thief had taken her to the richest part of Glenbard. The merchants mostly lived in the Northeastern section of the city, nearest the exit to Glenbard. Grace watched the thief sneak into private offices under the cover of darkness. Grace attempted to peek into the homes and though it was dark, it looked as if most were well-furnished. Many of them had small houses built nearby for servants' quarters.

The thief climbed through a window to the largest house in the merchant district. So far Grace saw nothing she hadn't been warned of. Ridley said the Thieves' Guild stopped stealing from their own class when Marcus took over, and even the drifter Kit stated the Guild kept murders within Glenbard down. Still, Jack spoke his piece on the morality (or lack thereof) of the Guild, making Grace doubt them. Her current thief turned up nothing, so for now The Death Dealer called it a night.

"That stall is filthy! Do it again!" Mayhew pushed the shovel and pail into Grace's hands.

To her, the stall looked clean. She wasn't sure what Mayhew wanted her to do to make it better, but she went right back in. Pilgrim looked up from his hay and blinked at her while Mayhew went to his corner to polish some saddles and bridles.

Grace patted Pilgrim's neck. "You think I do a fine job, don't you?" Pilgrim nipped at her pockets, looking for food.

Grace survived three days under Mayhew's command. It was a shock for everyone, causing no one to win the original bet set forth. However, now Grace's patience with Mayhew was waning and she was prepared to throw down her shovel and walk out. It was a tempting prospect, but self-preservation won out since Jim provided her with a free room above the stables to live in. He said all the stable hands had lived there, and since Grace seemed to be holding her own, he expected she'd want to move out of the tavern's inn. The biggest perk to living in the small room above the stables was that it was easier to sneak out at night for her nocturnal duties.

Grace spent her first night in the stables and found her window's exit was completely covered in shadows; making it easier to climb out without attracting attention. That night Grace trailed two more thieves and came up with nothing. The pattern suggested that each night Marcus sent out one thief to burglarize or vandalize a merchant's house. The men Marcus sent couldn't have been doing much damage, because the merchant class didn't hire goons to assault the Angel. Donald started making rounds around the marketplace for Grace during the days.

He noticed a few pickpockets whom he recognized as Marcus's men. Like the night thieves, they went after the most well-off people. Donald listened to the gossip and surmised that people generally didn't even know they were robbed in the night.

Watching the thieves was getting Grace nowhere and she longed to be back out as the traditional Death Dealer. Since gaining her first knowledge of the Guild, she had been formulating a plan on how to deal with them. Tonight she would set the plan into action. With any luck, before the sun rose she would have something worked out with the thieves.

Grace propped her shovel up against the stall door and cracked her back. Her stomach rumbled a bit, but Mayhew didn't like her asking to go to lunch. He liked to control her life while she worked during the days. She lifted the shovel again and exited Pilgrim's stall. She'd just have to wait for Mayhew's permission.

~*~*~

The thief's name was Roddy, and he was heading quickly toward the merchant district. As he moved through the dark of the night, a figure darted in front of him. Roddy stopped; unsure if the lights of one of Glenbard's taverns were playing tricks on him. Nothing moved in the shadows, so he continued on his way. Just as he started walking again, he saw something shift in the darkness. He stopped once more, positive he saw something.

Out of the shadows, a small figure moved. "You." The voice was soft, strained. Roddy moved his hand toward his dagger. "I have questions."

"Who are ya?" A hooded, black clad person moved into Roddy's line of sight. "The Death Dealer?"

"I need you to answer some questions, thief. How exactly does Marcus run the Fishermen's Collective?"

"He was poor in his youth and 'e don't want no one to suffer like him and 'is family did. So we's always steal from those that can afford it, or that cause trouble down in the lower city. Then we's give a portion to a fund Marcus uses to keep the widows and their babes clothed and fed. So Death Dealer, you needn't worry about us harming folk. I know 'ow you are about that. People who stir up things have a funny habit of disappearing from Glenbard."

"I want to speak to Marcus." The Death Dealer took a step closer to Roddy and he saw the glint of a sword. "Tonight. And I want you to bring him to me."

"I won't let you 'urt my king."

"I won't hurt him. I want to talk to him." The Death Dealer

tossed a bag to Roddy and the thief bent down; never letting his eyes stray from the drawn sword. The bag had a fair amount of coppers in it. "Bring Marcus to the temple of Diggery by two. I have business to discuss with him." Having said her piece, The Death Dealer deftly returned to the shadows.

~*~*~

Marcus brought his right hand man, Thom, to the temple, even though Roddy didn't seemed particularly spooked. He showed the bag of coins to Marcus, and Marcus and Thom tested the money to make sure it was good. Once they were satisfied, they returned it to Roddy. The King of Thieves was hesitant to go, but he didn't want The Death Dealer obstructing his work every night. Do-gooders always managed to do just that.

Inside the temple, The Death Dealer stood before the wolf statue of Diggery. Most of the flames were extinguished; either by those who maintained the temple or by this vigilante.

"Roddy said you accosted him in the dark." Marcus kept a hand on his sword hilt, and with one call Thom would be inside to help. The Death Dealer's sword was laid out on the altar.

"Stepping from the shadows is hardly accosting, but getting Roddy was the only way to bring you out of the Angel."

"And what does the hero of the people want with me? You surely can't expect to bring me down so the righteous will rule the day."

The Death Dealer was silent a moment. "Don't be daft. King Frederick has not brought you down yet, and he has an army at his disposal. I am only one person. I come to you for another reason. I have been watching your men and I questioned Roddy as to your intentions. You certainly are the honest thief they claim you to be."

"If you refer to my philosophy regarding poor children, no one should be unable to feed their children because of a lack of coin."

"I agree, and I see we have a common goal." The Death Dealer's soft voice dropped even lower. "We both want the people of Cesernan taken care of, so I propose an alliance. I certainly could never take you down, but people love a hero and that's what I am. If you killed me, it would only hurt your reputation as a good thief. I know you usurped the previous king for your crown, and I also know of your fund for the survival of widows; a most honorable venture. However, I can see to it that someone takes your crown if you deviate from your current path."

"You're threatening me?"

"I am simply keeping you mindful of what has happened to other leaders in the Thieves' Guild. But if you keep to the role of honest thief and take care of your own, I will be ever vigilant to stop any who come to take your title."

"How do you propose something like that? You can't be everywhere at once."

"No, and even my extra sets of eyes have limits. But what I do unearth, I can stalk and see to it that they never reach you or your throne."

Marcus put his hands on his hips. "You are making quite an assumption, here." The Death Dealer waited for an elaboration. "You think I want your help; that I need your help. You are sneaky, that is clear, but you are not invincible. What makes you so sure I won't have you killed?"

"As I said, many of your thieves think I am powerful enough and respectable enough. I could be a valuable ally while I am here in Glenbard. I can clear out rogue thieves and murderers outside the city, saving you time and energy. Together, the people will view us both as heroes."

"I need a sign I can trust you."

The Death Dealer took up the sword from the altar. He pointed to Marcus's dagger, which was tucked within his boot. "A blood oath. A prick on our palms and the mingling of blood. I have heard only terrible stories of those who violate blood oaths."

Marcus removed his dagger and made a small cut on the palm of his hand. Grace did the same. They clasped hands; sealing their oath. People were always threatening Marcus's power. While none had yet come with any true force, fighting them all back could be daunting. People were always buzzing about The Death Dealer, and petty criminals nearly wet themselves at the mere mention of his name. That kind of backing could keep some of the trash away from Marcus's seat of power.

So it was done. Whether Marcus was comfortable allying himself with The Death Dealer or not, it no longer mattered. The two were bound by their own blood. If Marcus failed to withhold his tradition as an honest thief, The Death Dealer would find someone who would. And in return, The Death Dealer would stay out of Guild affairs; letting the thieves do as they needed. Both parties would watch out for one another as best they could and see that no one attempted to destroy the other.

The next day in the tavern was hectic. The talk was all about The Death Dealer's visit, but Marcus didn't betray what transpired. Neither did Grace, even when Donald begged to know. For the time being, the nature of the agreement stayed between the King of Thieves and The Death Dealer.

Seven

The next week passed quickly in Glenbard. Grace made friends with many of the thieves in the Guild through Ridley's intervention. Marcus warmed to Grace, and even let her join his table for the evening meal. Even Donald found his way into the thief King's favor. Each day as Grace worked hard to impress Mayhew, Donald went about doing odd jobs here and there. Oftentimes, members in the Guild would send him on errands to run fresh bread or fruit to their families or to deliver messages to any ships that were in port. Over dinner, Grace and Ridley encouraged Donald to take a position on a trade ship and sail to the Nareroc Islands, and he continued to say no. Grace knew why, but Ridley only assumed it was because Donald had fallen in love with a merchant's daughter or something of the sort.

During the nights, Grace went out her bedroom window as The Death Dealer and patrolled the streets for trouble. Rumors quickly spread that The Death Dealer had come to Glenbard to become the new King of Thieves. Marcus publicly scoffed at this, but kept his secret about meeting with The Death Dealer. In any case, more and more people went to the temple of Diggery to thank her for protecting them by allying Marcus to The Death Dealer. Ridley began to get delusions of one day meeting The Death Dealer and possibly even marrying him, and Grace never tried to change Ridley's mind. She would just smile as her friend talked about it.

Although Grace didn't speak to Jack after the incident in the stable, she saw him every day sulking in his corner. He would come into the stables often enough to take Pilgrim out for exercises, but she never went to say anything and he did likewise to her. Grace never told anyone what he said. Many figured she just hated his negative attitude and didn't try to convince her otherwise. Donald would talk to him every so often; asking how long he was a stable hand and what he thought of the knights who were there before he left the position.

Things finally seemed to be going right in Grace's life until one unfortunate night.

Grace often traveled out of Glenbard to hide along the roadside and wait for troublemakers. It was almost always quiet and boring. The Guild kept the people in the city relatively safe, considering most were family members of those in the Guild. Any trouble that started usually took place on the country road leading to Glenbard, so each night Grace walked a mile out of town and spent a few hours patrolling about before returning for sleep.

On this unfortunate night, Grace was watching and waiting. Two men had kidnapped a young girl and were camped not far from the city limits; about a ten minute walk for her. Grace would have struck already but these men were huge, and she suspected they would be too much for her. She would have to wait until one nodded off. That way, she could dispose of the one on guard duty and knock him unconscious before he could raise the alarm.

The bigger of the two finally laid out his blankets and went to sleep. When he started snoring, Grace sneaked up behind his companion. She would have knocked him out successfully, except her shadow gave her away.

"Mac, wake up!" Grace panicked and hit the man over the head with the hilt of her sword. He lay in the dirt, unconscious.

The other man awakened instantly and was obviously angry. "The Death Dealer, huh? Awfully small, aren't you? And I bet you want to save this girl." He looked at the girl, whose hands were tied and her mouth gagged. "Well, you failed." The man pulled a knife and Grace lunged at him, but he was faster. The knife pierced the girl's heart so quickly, she didn't even have a chance to scream. "It's just you and me now."

Grace took a fighting stance, raised her sword, and they circled each other. Grace felt she had an advantage with her sword, but she was very wrong. The man was incredibly fast for someone so big. He jumped at Grace and grabbed her wrist with his free hand, pulled her close, and took one stab at her.

Although she twisted away from him, she wasn't quick enough to completely miss his knife. Blood dripped freely from her side. Using every bit of strength left in her, she cracked the man upside the head with her sword hilt and staggered away as he lay motionless by the fire.

The world spun around her as the dead man with the broken nose swirled around her mind. The memory of the sound of his nose cracking against her skull rang in her ears. Then she looked at the poor girl, dead and bleeding in the dirt. Grace no longer wanted to witness death. She vomited next to the fire; her throat burning as the bile surged upward.

~*~*~

Grace climbed into Donald's window and collapsed next to him on his bed. He quickly rose and lit a few candles, and then he saw Grace on her back, bleeding all over his covers.

"I need to get you some help." Grace still had The Death Dealer hood on. Her eyes drooped and she moaned slightly.

"No," she gasped. "No, there is no one! We cannot let Jim or Ridley or even Marcus know about this."

Cassandra always had a plan in case Grace was hurt; always had a lie at the ready to tell the healers. Donald had no such plan or lie. He panicked, and as he left the room he said, "I'm going to get someone!"

It was late, and of the few people who still loitered in the common room, they were either the drunks or the ladies trying to get money from them. Donald knew he couldn't tell Jim. Jim Little was a nice fellow, but he told everyone everything he knew. If he brought Jim to see Grace now he would know her secret, and by the time the sun rose, so would everyone else in Glenbard. Then both Donald and Grace's safety would be compromised.

Donald entered the common room and saw Jim, as well as a few people he didn't know. All were filled with ale. Then he spotted Jack in the corner. He knew Grace hated Jack, but there was no time to find someone else. Jack had never told anyone about Grace, so he had to be good at keeping secrets. Plus, he was strong and would be able to help move Grace. Donald hurried over, out of breath as he stood before Jack's table.

"A little late for knight talk, don't you think?"

"Jack, I need your help." Jack raised an eyebrow. "This is

urgent. Please?"

"Then have Jim help you."

"I can't. Please – there's no time to get Marcus or Ridley. Just help me, I beg you."

He had no real desire to help the young man, but Jack met Donald's eyes and looked at the fear within. He wasn't entirely sure what could be wrong so late, but he gave in.

"Make this quick, boy."

~*~*~

Jack opened Donald's door and saw a figure, clad in black with an executioner's hood on, lying on the bed. The Death Dealer was wounded and, more importantly, was passed out on Donald's bed. Jack could barely believe his eyes.

Jack walked over to the bed and sat beside the figure. He gently removed the hood and blonde locks fell out over the pillow. "Grace?" The girl moaned, but had already left the conscious world from blood loss.

Jack removed her jerkin and lifted the black shirt where the wound was. It wasn't deep and didn't hit any organs, but it still had the potential to be fatal, especially if they didn't find a healer. Jack wasn't going to let that happen. Despite his own feelings toward the girl, he knew it was wrong to just let her die.

He hoped Grace had extra covering on underneath as he ripped the shirt off her. He was relieved to see the girl had bound her chest. He looked closely at the laceration. The best thing to do would be to move Grace to a healing house, and fast.

"Where was she?"

"She sneaks out of the city. She told me once she doesn't go further than a mile or so."

"She walked a mile?" He continued to inspect the wound. "It's not deep, but it's long. The wound itself isn't fatal, but if she traveled the distance you claim, she's been bleeding for a while now."

Taking the ripped shirt, he tied it around the wound to slow the bleeding. Donald remained in the corner, panicking, and was useless to Grace now. Jack removed his jacket, put it on Grace, and then lifted her gently from the bed and carried her to the door.

"Make yourself useful and open the doors for us."

Donald did as he was told and opened the door so Jack could get out. He followed Jack and opened any other doors that presented a problem.

~*~*~

Jack brought Grace to the temple of Kamaria. The only indication they were in the house of the goddess was the silver crescent moon that hung above the door. When Grace awakened, she saw that she was in the back room where the priestesses prepared for the ceremonies to the moon goddess. Jack watched her with interest from the corner. As Grace sat up, she winced and gritted her teeth.

Jack could tell she was confused and didn't blame her. She had woken up in a strange room with strange clothes on. Taking a deep breath, she winced again.

"The wound was not fatal. Though it could have been if Donald had listened to you. The priestesses had to stitch you up."

Grace's eyes met Jack's hazel ones. He leaned on the back wall and watched her carefully. "You? *You're* the help Donald found?"

"I am afraid so."

"I suppose I should thank you, then."

"You don't have to if you don't want to. I know you're still angry with me."

"But you probably just saved my life." She suddenly blushed and quickly pulled the jacket closed around her body; noticing that her shirt had been cut away.

Jack rolled his eyes. "The healers cut your bindings, so your modesty is still intact. I didn't see anything. And you don't need to repay me or thank me. I just did what most would have done."

Grace's face contorted and her eyes widened as though she just remembered something important. *What could he have said to explain the gash?*

Jack took a guess at her thoughts and smiled at her for the first time. "The healers here have taken a vow of silence and

97

speak only when the moon is at her fullest. But they seemed to care little for what you did. They cared more for the safety of a fellow human. So your little secret is safe."

"And you? Can I trust you?"

"Does anyone here know you were once a noble?"

"No."

"Then your secret is safe with me."

Grace swung her legs over the bedside and suddenly felt lightheaded.

Jack went to her side and forced her back onto the bed. "It is best to stay here and rest. You lost too much blood." He wrapped the blankets of the bed around her shoulders.

"Mayhew will be furious with me if I am not in the stables by sunup." She attempted to cast off the offered blankets.

"It's well past noon, now. Donald took over for you, saying you were too ill to work. As far as anyone is concerned, last night Donald and I rushed you to see a healer about a fever and you're recovering here."

"Well I'm up now; can I go back to my room?"

Jack sighed. Arguing with Grace was going to be a losing battle. She was quite a willful young woman. "You can't walk all the way back there. You simply will not have the strength or energy." Grace huffed and crossed her arms over her chest; rolling her eyes in annoyance.

Jack let a little chuckle out. He had never met someone so stubborn when it came to accepting help after an injury. Not even the most arrogant of knights were this bad. Donald filled him in on the other times Grace had hurt herself and tried to simply walk it off. "If you're just going to get out of that bed when my back is turned, at least let me help you. I can bring Pilgrim here and you can ride him while I walk back to the Angel. But only if you promise to go straight to bed when we get back."

"I suppose I can do that."

Jack nodded and headed for the door.

"Jack?" He turned and caught a smile from Grace. "Thank you."

"Just don't tell anyone about me being so nice to you. If anyone asks, say I forced you to come back to the tavern and I was absolutely beastly." Grace looked dumbfounded. "They'll think I'll do favors for them, and I simply cannot let that happen."

Grace laughed and shook her head. "No, I don't suppose you can."

~*~*~

Grace was propped up on her pillows, watching Donald pace her little room. He was working in the stables when Jack brought her back to the Angel. Though Donald wanted to leave to help her, Mayhew was insistent he do the job Grace was hired to do.

Donald had been awarded his midday meal, but stood pacing in her room instead. "I know you hate Jack, but there was no other choice." Her friend seemed to think she would be furious that Jack's help had been enlisted.

"Why are you fretting so much? I can't be upset with you for saving my life. I'm just surprised he even helped."

Donald stopped his pacing to take a seat at the foot of her bed. "He stayed with me at the temple until dawn, and when I left to make your excuses to Mayhew, he said he would wait so a familiar face would be there when you woke up. All morning I've tried to get information out of Mayhew about Jack, but he wouldn't say anything."

Grace had to admit she was surprised to wake up and find Jack waiting for her. However, he hadn't been coarse with her; rather he was gentle, in his own sarcastic way. He even helped her into bed and saw to it that she had everything she needed. Then without a word, he left.

"Since Jack knows everything now, I was thinking..." Donald paused before continuing, "Maybe I *will* take a job on one of the merchant ships. I nearly lost my head last night and could do nothing but panic. Jack was sensible and was able to think clearly enough to take you to healers under a vow of silence. If he agrees, I will try to find work on a merchant ship. I've asked around; the pay isn't great, but you mostly live on the ship so room and board is taken care of."

99

"This is wonderful news." Grace held her arms open so Donald could hug her. His embrace hurt her wounds, but she refused to let him know. If he thought he hurt her, he'd be morose the rest of the day. His choice was good news. She couldn't let Donald just sit around doing odd jobs just to keep her safe.

~*~*~

Ridley brought Grace her dinner that night. "Jack, of all people, to take you to the healers. You poor thing! You look so tired. That fever came on so quickly."

"I felt rather ill all day." Grace hated lying to anyone, especially this trusting young woman, but it couldn't be helped. All day she thought about Jack and what Donald said about him waiting at the temple for her to wake up. Donald wasn't able to get any information from Mayhew, but she figured tapping into Ridley's gossip-filled brain would be worth a shot. "And Jack, well, I can't thank him enough. If not for him, the fever might have claimed me."

"It is very unlike him." Ridley broke apart a piece of bread.

"Why? What can you tell me about Jack?"

Ridley chewed her food, swallowed and shrugged. "He lives in a rundown little room by the Emerald Rose. When he arrived in Glenbard almost eight years ago, he was angry, fearless, and most often drunk. That's why they say he became a rusher at the Rose. He had some sort of death wish. He made a name for himself cracking skulls, breaking elbows, and making problems disappear. After a month as a rusher, Marcus took notice. He thought Jack was a rogue from outside Cesernan. He sent spies out from here to Eurur and as far as Archon, trying to gain knowledge. No one had ever heard the name Anders.

"He no longer works as a rusher, but he has gold from somewhere. No one knows where his money comes from. According to his landlady, she reduces payments because he keeps ruffians out. That's all anyone really knows. He's always kept to himself, living in the present rather than talking about the past. After a few years, everyone gave up guessing his origins. He wasn't here to take the King of Thieves' crown, so they left him

100

alone."

"So he just appeared one day?"

Ridley nodded. "It's best to let Jack be. He'll talk when he wants." She grinned mischievously. "I suppose if I ask about your interest in Jack, you'll claim it's only because he helped you last night." She winked and Grace blushed.

Jack was surly and standoffish, yet he helped get her to a healer. Not only that, but he also kept her secrets. He was a confusing man, and she intended to crack his shell so she could understand him.

Eight

Grace stayed in her room for the next week based on the orders of Donald. Every night Ridley and Marcus came up to her room with dinner and chatted for a bit, and then they would leave so she could rest. Donald had already set out for his first job in the islands, since the captain said he was willing to take on any man foolish enough to want it so badly.

With a hug and a lecture, Donald left. He figured if Jack could be trusted, then Grace was in more capable hands than his own. Grace missed him, but knew he'd be back before she even knew he was gone.

Jack was scarce after he returned Grace to the Angel from the temple. It was not until the night Grace planned to rejoin everyone in the common room that Jack finally paid her a visit.

The two had come to a quiet understanding the day after Grace was stabbed, and the walk back to the tavern was pleasant for both. Their friendship had limits, and both were willing to respect them if the other did as well. So when Jack broke their unspoken agreement and came to see her at her room over the stables, Grace was quite surprised.

She was fixing her hair when Jack knocked and peered in. "Hello Jack, please come in."

Jack slipped in and closed the door. "The tournament is over, and the merchants from Glenbard who went to see it and sell their goods have returned. They brought back not only profits, but stories as well. The big story this year is about a woman who stepped into the sword ring and was subsequently exiled from the court. Of course, this little bit of news has been floating around for weeks. A witch of terrible girth disguised herself to belittle the Prince. A red-eyed harpy planned to murder the royal family. But now, more concrete information has been provided. A member of Arganis's noble family; a small, blonde-haired young woman is the one who took up the sword."

"So? Who really cares?" Grace turned back to her mirror and tried to fix her braids.

Jack firmly took hold of her shoulders and turned her to face him. "Everyone cares, Grace. Jim, Ridley, and even Marcus could still care for you, but not everyone will be so happy to have a former noble walking around Glenbard in the common room of their favorite inn. They complain that King Frederick and his cronies sit at banquet while they starve. More than one of noble birth has been assaulted in dark places, and let's not forget how the King taxes his people. These may be exaggerated rumors from the dissatisfied masses, but they believe all this to be fact. They hate people like you, Grace."

Grace saw a flicker of concern in Jack's eyes as he spoke. "I wouldn't go in that common room tonight. Tell Ridley privately and see how she reacts, but there could be trouble if you dare enter that room tonight and are recognized. And you *will* be recognized. I'm not going to be around to help you."

"You don't think I can handle myself, do you? You, of all people, should know I can take care of myself."

"Take care of yourself? Look at you! You're an ex-noble who likes to play hero. You'll get yourself killed if you go into that common room tonight!" Jack released Grace and shook his head. He could tell by the way she looked at him that she was going down there tonight anyway. He tried; that was all that mattered. "Have it your way."

He stomped across the room and made sure to slam the door as he left. Grace sat and stewed in her anger for a few minutes before deciding it was time to head down for supper in the tavern. Jack was wrong; no one would really care. She wasn't a noble anymore. Now she mucked out stables for a living.

~*~*~

Grace headed into the common room and no one seemed to notice her until Ridley declared her entrance. "Everyone! Grace is on the mend and she's come to join us!" Those who knew Grace cheered, but a few men kept their eyes downward and spoke amongst each other.

Finally, one stood up as a group of tavern regulars went to see Grace. "You cheer this woman? This child who once lived in

103

luxuries that we'll never know? You are a tramp, Lady Grace Hilren of Arganis!" He spat out her former title.

"What are you talking about, Van?" Marcus asked from his seat of power by the fireplace. "Grace here mucks out the stables for Mayhew."

"Does she, indeed?" the man named Van asked; crossing the tavern floor to look more closely at Grace. "This girl was the former noblewoman we were talking about. It's people like *her* that keep us down! And now she steals a job from someone who actually needs it."

Those who came to wish Grace well backed away from her in fear and suspicion or disgust and anger. She looked around to see many angry eyes fall on her; eyes that were happy she was well only moments before. This was the second time in recent memory that a crowd had suddenly turned so viciously on her. The masses were a fickle beast.

"Is it true, Grace?" Ridley's voice came from next to her. She turned and the Princess of Thieves was only two feet away.

Grace hung her head. "Yes, it is true."

"She's not one of ours! Throw her out!" someone yelled.

"Slit her throat and send her head back to the court! Show them what we do to those who belong there!" another voice cried out.

Grace caught the glint of steel from the corner of her eye and turned to Ridley. The girl produced a dagger and held it out. For a moment she thought Ridley had turned on her as well.

"How dare you! You call yourselves men! You would dare to cast out and hurt someone who has become one of ours? Grace Hilren may have been born a noble, but she works like a commoner. She works like one of us! And if any one of you dares to touch her, I'll slice your hands off!"

Ridley moved to Grace's side and brandished her dagger at the angry mob. She produced a second one from her belt and prepared for a fight. As the crowd began to advance on the women, Marcus rose from the corner and stood on his chair.

"You fools will resort to violence over this? Look what

you're doing – picking a fight with two women. Have you no honor? That dog Frederick spits on us and shows disrespect to a girl with fire and heart, and now you would all do the same?"

A few men backed down at Marcus's words, but there were those who did not. A giant hand grabbed Grace's braid and pulled her into him while at the same time, Ridley was taken in a frontal assault by Van. Those who were closest to Marcus rushed to Ridley and Grace's aid, including Jim the innkeeper. Marcus jumped down from his chair and fought to get through the crowds.

Grace elbowed her attacker hard in the stomach and his grip loosened. She was able to pull away, but more were waiting to challenge her. Most involved in the fight had daggers or knives as weapons. In Arganis the weapons master believed dagger and knife fighting was unrefined, and as a knight Calvin would never need it, so it was never taught. Now Grace wished she had learned even a little. In these close quarters, a sword would do harm to friend and foe alike.

Another man took Grace by the wrist and pulled her against him. "Come on, my lady – my fair *noblewoman* – fight back." Grace kicked with all her might and booted her attacker in his shin; horrified to learn the leg she just kicked was wooden. She kicked his other shin and although he winced for a moment, he did not loosen his grip; he only pulled her closer. Grace had never fought dirty in her life, but she knew where the weak spots were on men and now she didn't hesitate to take full advantage. "I've never had a noblewoman before."

"And you won't tonight, either." Grace kicked harder than the two times before and made contact in the man's groin. His face went deathly white and then bright red. He toppled over, still gripping Grace's wrist.

She went down and banged her head on a table as she went. She winced in pain but was able to get free. Feet moved all about her and Grace knew any second she would find herself under someone's boot. She closed her eyes and prayed for a miracle.

One strong arm scooped her off the floor and back onto her

feet. "You just don't listen, do you?" Grace was never as happy to hear Jack's voice as she was at that moment. Jack pulled Grace close to him and kept a sword drawn, but the fighting died down.

Grace remembered that Jack was famous around Glenbard as a rusher, and his legendary skills must have frightened some of the ruffians. Kit stood next to him with a dagger, and she sliced the man who tackled Ridley and prepared to do it again. Where they came from, Grace didn't care. She only cared that Kit was no stranger with a weapon in her hand and Jack supported her. As it was, she felt as if her knees were going to give out. Her head pounded and a wave of nausea washed over her.

Jim Little emerged from the crowd, pulling Van and another man by the collars. "Start a fight in my tavern, will you?" He dragged them all the way to the door and threw them roughly into the streets. "Don't ever come back to the Angel again!"

Marcus appeared with a bruised Ridley at his side and they came straight for Grace, Jack and Kit. Grace was shaking from the adrenaline rush and because she was afraid others would still try to come after her. She also worried that if Jack let her go, she'd simply sink to the floor. Luckily he kept a firm arm around her waist. He obviously knew better than to let her go. Jim joined them.

"Everyone all right?" the innkeeper said as he looked around. A few broken plates and some knocked-over tables and chairs, but nothing the Angel Tavern and Inn hadn't seen before.

"A bit bruised, it looks like," Marcus said; taking stock of the injuries. Ridley's left hand had been nicked and there was a large red mark swelling on her cheek. Grace's head throbbed and a similar red mark was forming on her forehead. Tomorrow she and Ridley would have impressive bruises.

"We're lucky you came along when you did, Jack." Jim nodded to Jack and Kit. "And you as well, young lady."

Grace sighed. "I think I need to go out for some air."

"Do you ever learn your lesson?" Jack growled by her ears.

"Those fools will still be milling about, girlie," Marcus said.

"I'll go with her," Kit said. "The air in here is stifling and I need some fresh air myself. This is not the time to be walking about alone." She sheathed her dagger and took over supporting Grace.

~*~*~

At first Kit and Grace did not speak. They just walked side by side toward the temple district. People stared, some whispered angrily, but no one bothered them. Grace headed into Diggery's temple and took a seat up front near the statue of the wolf Diggery.

"Maybe everyone is right and I really don't belong here."

"Oh? You have certainly made a name for yourself in less than an hour. Where would you go, if not here?"

"You have traveled the world…where do you suggest?"

Kit's purple eyes glinted in the soft candlelight of the temple and she stared thoughtfully upon Grace. There was a deep wisdom hidden in the young face, and Grace wondered how someone so young obtained it.

"If you wish to go somewhere where outcasts are welcome, I suggest Archon. Refugees from many countries have found their way there to seek asylum from the harsh realities of this world. It is a place of learning and peace. Or if you want to go where women are more respected, I say head for Eurur. Some of King Christian's most trusted advisers are women, and in the provinces of Dorhedge and Morhollow, women are allowed to serve in the army."

"What about Sera? Have you ever been there?"

"Its people are proud of their land and proud of their traditions. They can be harsh to outsiders. Stubborn as well." She gave Grace a sly smile as she said that. "But if you really want to know what I think, you should stay in Cesernan. It is your home, after all, and think of all the friends you would be leaving behind if you left. You had a bad piece of luck tonight, but think about how so many were quick to accept you, even when your heritage was discovered. You already made one tragic, rash decision at the tournament…don't make another one by running away."

"Maybe you're right, but it seems rather useless to stay. Half

107

of Glenbard hates me as it is."

"That's not true, and even if it is, there are those who will not let harm come to you. Come on, now – you should get back to the Angel. We shouldn't have come as far with tempers so high, and the night draws on. You start mucking out stables again tomorrow, do you not?"

"Yes." Kit got to her feet and helped Grace up.

They walked back and shared a few pleasant words about the weather and this and that. Kit took Grace up to her room to bid her farewell, as she was heading out in the morning to the Nareroc Islands.

When they returned, Grace noticed that a candle on her desk had been lit and an ornate dagger was stabbed into the wood on her nightstand. There were strange symbols and a flowing script on the blade, and a dragon's head on the handle with two ruby jewels for the eyes. She pulled it from the wood and handed it over to Kit.

"Do you recognize the symbols at all?" Grace asked.

"This is from Escion. Do you know anyone from that province?"

Grace's thoughts went straight to Tristan, but she couldn't fathom why he would have left her a dagger. There was a small piece of parchment paper where the dagger was, and Grace picked it up to read.

Learn to use it or death will surely find you. Swordplay is no longer useful when fighting the damned.

Kit looked over Grace's shoulder. "It appears someone from Escion witnessed the fight this evening and wishes you well. Jack tells me the girl Ridley is quite good with knife play; perhaps you should see her about learning some yourself. Well, goodnight and good luck, Grace. I could be gone weeks or months. I am never sure when I will find my way back into Cesernan. Until next we meet." Kit and Grace bowed to one another and the wanderer disappeared out the door, leaving Grace alone to ponder the riddle of the dagger.

~*~*~

108

"You've only been gone a week and already you've gone soft from sickness!" Mayhew snapped as Grace dropped a large wooden bucket full of water.

Her injury from the knife flared to life and pain shot up her side as she tried to lift the bucket. It wasn't the first thing Grace dropped, and it was not even noon yet. Her head throbbed from the excitement of the night before and her Death Dealer wound had yet to fully heal.

"I am sorry, Master Mayhew," she said and picked the bucket up again; heading to fill it with water once more.

"No! I won't have you dropping another bucket! There's a new patron at the Angel; arrived a while back while you were piddling away with the water. Unsaddle his horse and brush it down. He paid me handsomely to make sure his horse is well looked after. Now get to it!"

Grace wasted no time and went straight to the stall Mayhew pointed toward. A massive gray stallion was waiting to be handled and he stamped his foot as Grace came near him. The stallion snapped angrily as Grace reached up to undo his bridle, and she idly thought about how this horse was better suited to Jack's personality than the well-mannered Pilgrim in the next stall.

"Easy, boy." Grace slowly reached up, unhooked the bridle and slipped it carefully from the horse's head. He watched her with angry eyes and shook his mane furiously when the bridle was off.

The last thing Grace needed was to be kicked by the angry beast, so with great care and caution she began working on the saddle. Pilgrim put his head over the stall wall and sniffed at the new stallion, but the horse did not take kindly to it and neighed wildly; snapping at poor Pilgrim. Jack's horse and Grace both jumped, and when Grace looked back, she saw that the saddle was only half off.

Now it slid around on the horse's back and the saddle part hung loosely to one side. She gave a heavy sigh and cautiously attempted to get the saddle off once more. This time all the beast did was stamp his front hooves angrily. Finally, Grace slid the saddle off and slung it over the stall wall. She wasn't looking forward to brushing the stallion down.

Mayhew came over. "What's the damn commotion over here?"

"I'm sorry sir, but this horse is ill-tempered and snaps at everything I do."

Mayhew handed Grace a brush. "Brush him down and let me see."

With soft, slow steps Grace approached the horse once more. It was perfectly still, waiting for something, and Mayhew watched as Grace brushed the horse down. At first he thought the girl was lying, but suddenly the horse swung his head around and snapped at Grace. She jumped out of the way just in time to narrowly miss his powerful teeth.

"Get out of the stall, girl." Mayhew yanked the brush from Grace. "I won't have you out sick again because that beast kicks you. You make sure the other horses have water and food and then go get some lunch yourself. I'll finish with this demon horse."

~*~*~

Grace dragged herself into the common room of the Angel. She carried a plate from the cook and slumped down at Jack's usual table.

"Tough morning with Mayhew?" Jack pulled his pipe from his mouth and blew out a smoke ring.

"Tough day with some newcomer's horse. It was the most ill-tempered thing I ever met."

"You must be talking about that man, then." Jack pointed the end of his pipe toward a burly man talking to Marcus.

Grace looked over her shoulder and gasped when she caught a glimpse of the stranger's face. She quickly turned back to Jack and took in a few deep breaths. "It's him, Jack," she whispered.

"Him who?"

"The man who stabbed me."

Jack looked at the man again. "Are you sure?"

110

"Positive. What's he doing here? Who is he?"

"I cannot answer those questions for you, but it would be best to ask Marcus when you have the chance. Don't worry though; he won't recognize you, even though you recognize him."

"That doesn't matter. He kidnapped a girl, killed her in cold blood right in front of me, and tried to do the same to me. I have to know who he is."

"Don't go looking for trouble again, Grace. He bested you once and he can undoubtedly do it again."

Grace ignored her hunger and Jack's warning and rose from her seat; slowly crossing the room to stand before Marcus.

"Ah, and who is this lovely thing, Marcus? You keepin' her a secret from me? Want her all to yourself, do you?"

"Mac Cooper, allow me to introduce Grace Hilren. Grace, this is Mac, a member of the Thieves Guild. He watches my interests elsewhere in Cesernan."

Grace could not believe this man was in the Guild. Guild members didn't kidnap and kill helpless women for no reason on the side of the road. Not the Guild members she consorted with.

Mac rose, took Grace's hand and kissed it. "A pleasure to find someone so beautiful waiting in Glenbard for my return. Marcus, you didn't have to get me such a present."

Grace turned her head and saw Jack watching intently from his corner. He looked annoyed at Mac's attention toward Grace. She slowly pulled her hand away and took a few steps back.

"Grace mucks out the stables for Mayhew. She's no present of yours, Mac," Marcus said with a laugh. "But if you'll excuse us Grace, we have business that needs tending to."

Grace bowed to the King of Thieves and walked back to Jack's table.

~*~*~

That evening before going to dinner, Grace asked Ridley to show her a bit of knife play. Ridley was like a demon possessed with her daggers. Grace was impressed with how well she handled them and how she managed to hit the target's bulls-eye when she threw. Grace tried hard to keep up with Ridley, but she was too used to the sword techniques she learned in Arganis.

After an hour of trying to keep up with Ridley, the girl called a halt. "Grace, keep lower to the ground. You aim too high. This isn't like sword fighting; this is more of a hit-and-dodge type of fighting. If you really want to learn, meet me out here every night before dinner and we'll practice. I'm starving now though, so let's go in and get some dinner."

"Let's eat down on the pier. We can ask Jim to wrap us up some supper."

"What's wrong with the common room?"

"If you join me down on the pier, I can explain." Grace didn't want to express her distrust of Mac until she was far away from the ears of the Angel.

~*~*~

Ridley was finishing off the flagon of wine and Grace had yet to tell her anything. Grace was oddly evasive of Ridley's questions, and the Princess of Thieves wondered what had come over her friend.

Finally Grace opened up. "What can you tell me about Mac?"

"Mac Cooper? What's he got to do with anything?"

"I'm not sure I trust him, that's all."

"No one trusts him. Marcus sent him abroad to get him away from Glenbard and Mac's false claim as king of the Guild. He tries to make it seem as though he trusts him, but he's wary of Mac. No one else can even stand the man, but no one speaks openly of it. Most of the Guild thinks Marcus and Mac are good friends. But I know the truth, and so do a few of Marcus's closest allies. Everyone is on their toes now that Mac has returned."

"Why is he back?"

Ridley looked around and lowered her voice; drawing closer to Grace. "This is being kept extremely quiet, but Marcus's cousin was kidnapped a while back. Marcus contacted Mac to see if he knew anything, and Mac was on his way here to report his findings. But about a week ago Mac found the girl's body on the side of the road, and she was next to the body of a man. Mac believes The Death Dealer killed the kidnapper after he had killed

Marcus's cousin. Marcus is very distressed, but he's trying not to let it show."

Grace put her head down. She had doomed Marcus's cousin to death by trying to help her. "I think Mac is lying."

"I think you're right, but Marcus believes him on this. Mac even showed Marcus the bodies, but I think there's more to this tale than he is letting us know. No one speaks openly of this, although a few around the inn know. You cannot let anyone else know."

"My lips are sealed. So what are you going to do about Mac?"

"Nothing yet; I just hope he leaves soon. Stay away from him. He's trouble, and make no mistake."

"I have no intention of being near Mac."

"Maybe not, but trouble seems to find you."

What Ridley said gave Grace a lot to ponder. She thought about visiting Marcus again as The Death Dealer, but it would be dangerous with Mac in the city. Her promise to Marcus was to see to it that no one usurped his crown, and it seemed that was probably what Mac intended. There was no telling how much support Mac had in as well as out of Glenbard, and if she forced his hand now it could end horribly for herself and her new friends. For now she'd have to watch and wait. Her only concern was that when she did move, she'd be too late.

~*~*~

Grace stayed away from the common room of the Angel for a few days and worked hard to stay out of sight as she mucked out the stalls. At night, she and Ridley went down to the pier to eat and practice. Though Grace tried to stay out of trouble, a few regulars at the inn still glared at her when she brushed through for her meals. For the most part they trusted her because Marcus didn't mind her being a former noble, but a few still held a grudge. None made any move against her because of her friendship with the Thieves' Guild, but she still kept her guard up in case anyone was fool enough to come after her.

She felt strong enough to return to being The Death Dealer,

but there was little trouble on the roads. The festival for Ciro was fast approaching and most people kept the peace around that time. It was like that all over Cesernan, so Grace's days were filled with hiding from Mac and other angry patrons of the Angel, while her nights were spent wandering as The Death Dealer with no one to catch. But despite all her trying, Grace couldn't stay out of trouble for long.

Hammer, Mac's ill-tempered horse, and Mac had just returned from an early morning ride. Mac handed the reins over to Grace. "He needs looking after."

Mayhew had gone in for an early lunch and Grace hated the idea of looking after Hammer. Mayhew usually did it these days because he didn't want Grace getting wounded again. Now it would have to be Grace who unsaddled and brushed down the stallion. She wanted to stall for time, but it didn't seem to be a possibility.

Mac stood by and watched as Grace went into the stall where Hammer was waiting for her to unhook the bridle. Grace looked around for a sympathetic face, but the only one she found was Pilgrim's. The gelding was often tortured by nipping from Hammer and he fully understood what Grace was feeling.

As she reached out for the bridle, Hammer neighed furiously and snapped at her. Grace drew her hands back and stepped against the stall door. "My horse needs looking after *now*." Grace heard a mocking fury behind Mac's words, even though she couldn't see his expression.

"Sir, your horse hates me. Perhaps it would be best if I went to fetch Master Mayhew."

Grace reached behind her and felt for the door to push it open and get out of the stall. Mac grabbed her by the wrist and spun her around. "*You* do it!" His breath reeked of whiskey and his pupils danced; a clear sign he'd been drinking too much. Perhaps this early morning ride was just him returning after a night-long bender.

Mac let her go and pushed her backward toward Hammer.

Grace sucked up her courage. She had already survived

114

worse things in the world than an angry horse. Still, she reached up with shaking hands and reached once more for the bridle. Hammer snorted and stamped his hoof, and she closed her eyes and somehow managed to get the bridle off without the beast snapping at her. Pilgrim twitched nervously in his stall and looked past Grace and Mac to the door that led into the Angel. He whinnied and hung his head.

"Now the saddle."

"Please sir, let me get Mayhew. He is much better at taming your horse than I."

"I told *you* to do it." Grace moved to exit, but Mac closed the stall door on Grace and held it. "Or is the little noble girl afraid of a stallion? You used to geldings up at court?" The way Mac sneered, she knew he wasn't talking about his horse so much as himself.

Sighing but determined, she moved around Hammer and tried to unhook his saddle. The horse snorted and snapped at Grace's fingers, almost getting a hold of one. She pushed herself against the wall and felt her heart banging inside her chest. She looked over at Mac and met his glaring eyes. "Please, sir."

"Afraid of his teeth, are you? Here's somethin' to be afraid of." Mac whistled a high trill; the same that Calvin used to call the hounds in.

The stallion's ears flattened and he went mad at the noise; kicking angrily at the door and swinging his head back and forth. He kicked out his back hooves angrily and neighed loudly. It was all too close for comfort. Mac whistled again and Hammer continued his protest to the noise.

"Try to unsaddle him now!" Mac said with a laugh. Grace was as scared of that laugh as she was of the maddened beast.

Pilgrim neighed loudly in protest, as did a few other horses. Grace was afraid to turn her back on the raging Hammer, but she was even more terrified not to. She quickly turned and found a foothold in the wood of the wall and flung herself over into Pilgrim's stall. The wall was about five feet in height, and she landed on her right knee in something that hadn't yet been mucked out.

Springing to her feet, she glared at Mac. "You could have gotten me killed!"

She left Pilgrim's stall and stood before Mac. Although Grace was much smaller in comparison, she puffed out her chest and drew her shoulders back. Mac simply looked down at her and laughed. Angry at what he had done and hurt by the laugh, Grace drew a fist and hauled off and stopped Mac's laugh with one punch.

Clearly the hit was harder than he expected from her. She caught him right in the nose and a few droplets of blood trickled down onto his lips. She went in for another punch, but Mac caught her fist this time. He twisted it behind her back, but Grace refused to cry out in pain. If she didn't do something, she knew he would break it. Grace kept her glaring eyes on him, though; fighting back the tears and the scream. While he was distracted with making her cry, she used her free fist to hit his temple. Mac stumbled a little.

"Trying to be brave?" Mac released her and took a more direct road to making Grace hurt. She couldn't react in time to avoid Mac's fist as it made contact with her face. She remembered seeing it come at her and then she remembered the blood rushing down her face. Still, she refused to cry out. Pilgrim did that for her. The gelding was kicking his stall door to get at Mac.

The man threw her into the wall opposite Hammer's stall and held her there with one hand on her throat while the other hand worked to deflect her slaps and punches. He closed the gap between their bodies; the stink of his breath burning her nose, mixing with the smell of blood.

"You've a job to do. Take care of my horse or your final moments on this earth will consist of you struggling to breathe." She continued to beat her hands against him.

"It's not polite to strike a lady," Jack's calm voice came from the door to the Angel's common room. He always seemed to appear without making any noise.

"I know you loner, and this is none of your concern. I'm simply disciplining Mayhew's stable wench." Mac stopped and removed his hand from Grace's throat.

"Disciplining her in what? The proper care of a mad horse owned by a drunken thief who would disrespect a young woman and put her in danger?" Jack retorted, and Mac snarled.

"Jack." Grace held her bleeding nose and staggered forward. "I can handle him." She couldn't let Mac best her again, and with her eyes she pleaded with Jack to understand. She was finally free of Mac's grip, and if she made a move now, Mac would be unprepared.

Jack knew what Grace was doing. She told him one morning over breakfast she planned to get Mac and beat him. She said it was because she thought he was going to kill Marcus, but Jack knew it was more than that. She wanted revenge for the wound Mac had given her. However, Grace knew Jack had little faith in her. Mac was huge, drunk and angry. Trained as he was in self-defense, Jack didn't even know if *he* could best Mac. He was considered tall, but Mac was at least a head larger than he, with solid muscle packed in his body. There was no hope of Grace beating him, especially in a fist fight. Part of her knew it, but she was determined to try.

"Shut up, girl!" Mac prepared to reach for Grace again, but Jack threw all his weight into a tackle.

The two rolled around on the floor. The smart thing would have been for Grace to run and get help, but she didn't want to seem weak in the eyes of anyone. Those who still distrusted her would see this as her attempt to throw punishment on one of their own, though Mac had tried to kill her with his horse. Instead, Grace took up a bucket of water and threw it on the two wrestling men.

They stopped and Mac was the first to his feet. Grace was armed with the empty bucket, ready at any moment to hit him with it. He cast his eyes back to Jack. "I'll get you soon enough, Mad Dog Anders! You *and* this wench you bed." And he stormed out of the stables.

Jack was instantly at Grace's side. "Have you lost what little bit of sense you have left? He could have killed you, and for some reason you were stupidly content to let that happen!"

"I can take care of myself!" Grace caught Jack in the stomach with the bucket and stated, "I have work to finish." Jack didn't budge, so she screamed, "Get out!"

~*~*~

Mayhew returned to find a bruised and bloody-faced Grace. She explained that Mac's horse had gone mad, but she left out the rest of the details of the story. She sat alone, eating dinner in the tavern, and sat as far from Jack's usual table as possible. She even declined company from Ridley. She would have eaten in her room, but she wanted to hear if Mac said anything about the fight. To her relief, Mac and Jack both kept quiet about the origins of their wounds.

Grace pushed her plate away even though she'd barely touched any of her food. The fight with Mac left her disillusioned, yet again. He was strong; too strong for her. Still, Marcus's life could be at stake. Deep down, Grace knew it would be in everyone's best interest to have The Death Dealer visit Marcus again. However, that could prove to be as dangerous as going after Mac alone. She needed to get Mac's intentions and plans right first. Then she could go to Marcus.

Jack took a seat across from Grace and slid a bottle of ointment toward her. "For the bruises on your face and wrists." Grace said nothing. "Be angry if you want, but you're being stupid. Marcus already has people watching Mac. You need to focus your nightly energies elsewhere. You're not going to get him unless you stab him in his sleep, and you know how foolish *that* would be."

"I can't let him go unchecked."

"You concern yourself with Mac later – when you're stronger and are prepared to fight dirty. Now give me your wrist." Jack took Grace's wrist and rubbed some ointment into it. It smelled similar to what the castle healer had given her after her first kill, and she shuddered at the thought. A sea of blood washed over her

118

mind's eye.

Seeing that Grace was now entertaining guests, Marcus made his way over. Jack stopped what he was doing and gave his attention to the King of Thieves. He still held onto Grace's wrist, though. "I heard there was a bit of an accident in the stables today."

"I am far too clumsy sometimes." Grace gave Marcus a sheepish grin but he was unamused.

"And what is your excuse, Anders?"

"She's far too clumsy for my own good." Jack leaned back in his chair; finally letting go of Grace. He reached into his coat and retrieved his pipe.

"If I guess correctly, a drunken Mac may have had a hand in Grace's clumsiness." Neither Jack nor Grace wanted to reveal to Marcus what happened, however the King of Thieves had already made his assumptions on the matter. "Wouldn't be the first time he's caused an 'accident', and I doubt it will be the last. I can understand your silences, but I assure you the matter is being handled. I'll have no more 'accidents' among friends."

"How do you plan to stop them?" Jack said. "It's hard to punish clumsiness."

"Never you mind. If it happens again, let me know." And Marcus was gone.

A silence settled between Grace and Jack. His expression was unreadable and Grace wondered if Jack's mind was moving as fast as her own. "What do you think Marcus has planned?"

"My guess is he's rooting out Mac's followers first. There's no telling what kind of allies Mac has or what his intentions are. I suspect Marcus is like The Death Dealer. He's waiting for the right time, because it could be dangerous to move too soon." Grace nodded her agreement and Jack continued, "I'm going to caution you again to keep your nose clean. You've gained Mac's attention in too many ways now." Jack patted her hand before he rose and left.

Nine

At lunch the next day, Grace was completely exhausted. She tossed and turned most of the night, thinking of Mac, Marcus, and about Jack's cautions. What little sleep she did get barely helped in getting her through her morning chores in the stable. When lunch finally came around, she sat at the table next to Jack's and put her head down for a quick nap. She didn't even care about eating.

Jack put his feet up on the table and quietly watched Grace. He was not interested in company, but he said nothing. He just continued to smoke his pipe. If the girl wanted to sleep at his table, who was he to stop her?

The tavern was relatively dead until Ridley burst through the door. She was out of breath, but there was an enormous smile on her face. "You'll never guess what I just saw down at the pier!"

A few regulars looked at Ridley and made some off-hand jokes, and then Jim Little emerged from the kitchen and slung a dish towel over his shoulder. "Don't keep us guessing! What was down at the pier?"

"A great ship with tattered flags from Nareroc."

Someone threw a half-eaten potato at Ridley. She dodged it and it slapped against the wall. "You got our hopes up for something that happens all the time?"

"No, you fools! A Nareroc flag on a ship with a sea serpent's head carved into the bow." No one said anything. "Come on! The *Fearless Dawn* has returned!"

Grace lifted her head at this. The *Fearless Dawn* was a legendary pirate ship. The captain changed every few years, but the ship was a sailor's nightmare, or so she heard. Ravaging women, pillaging ships, fearing no Navy and holding the ability to create a mist to hide in, the stories grew every year. It raided the coast near Arganis more than once when she was growing up, but the incidents were not clear in her memory. Grace found the whole business exhilarating. She had kept The Death Dealer quiet recently because the Thieves Guild cleared out trouble, but with pirates abroad she could return to her beloved hood.

Jack groaned in his corner. "That means Kay is back."

Ridley pulled up a chair and sat between Grace and Jack's tables. "Don't be so harsh about Captain Kay."

"That woman is absolutely insane. She comes in here and starts fights, then leaves the Angel and all of Glenbard in a mess. I would rather see a pack of wild dogs run through here. Dogs, at least, do their business outside."

"This is your lucky day then, because Kay and some of the men from her crew are on their way. I'm going to go meet them outside." Ridley jumped up and rushed back out the door.

"Is this Kay woman really all that bad?" Grace asked.

"She can be. She comes in using Nareroc flags so the King's guard and the Navy won't bother her, and then she causes a big ruckus and leaves to plunder some helpless merchant ships or little coastline villages. She's my age, has been captain for over three years, and the crew seems to have become even more bloodthirsty under her."

"Ridley seemed quite taken by her."

"Yes. Kay Lansa is a hero to Ridley because she's unafraid. However, she's often unafraid and reckless."

Grace sighed. "She sounds interesting enough. Maybe you should give her another chance. She cannot be as bad as you say."

"There was a time we used to be friends, then she took to the sea and changed. But you'll see for yourself."

The wooden door of the Angel was suddenly thrown open. A woman of medium height walked through the door, with Ridley following. She had the dusky complexion of native women of Nareroc. Her skin was darker than Sir Edmund's was, because her blood wasn't diluted with that of Cesernan's nobility. She had thick, black hair tied back into a braid that fell to her mid-back. She kept a sword at her side, and Grace could make out the hilt of a dagger tied to her boot. About five men swarmed in behind her, each looking more grizzled and deadly than the last.

"Jim!" the woman called. "Drinks all around! The boys of the *Fearless Dawn* have returned and they're thirsty!"

121

The crew members of the *Fearless Dawn* bustled in and sat here and there, but Kay, with Ridley at her side, made straight for Jack.

"Jack Anders…still hanging around the Angel? Given any thought to my proposal?"

"I have no wish to join you, or those dogs you travel with at sea. There's no desire in me to be a pirate." Jack put his pipe up to his lips and blew a smoke ring at Kay.

"A fighter like you? I could use your bite on my crew. And I remember a time when you worked as an enforcer down by the docks. Busting skulls and breaking hands with the best." Kay pulled up a chair and sat across from Jack, and Ridley returned to her chair between tables. Kay completely ignored Grace, but even Ridley wasn't paying any mind to Grace.

"Jack's a lost cause, Kay. Me, on the other hand, I could be the best thing to happen to your ship," Ridley said and sat straight up. She was a fierce enough looking youth, but Grace knew her better. She giggled at the thought of Ridley being a bloodthirsty pirate.

"And who are you?" Kay asked, turning her attention for the first time to Grace. "Who dares to sit so close to Mad Dog Anders? I'd like to say his bark is worse than his bite, but, well…" Kay motioned toward one of her men. A long, white scar ran down his left cheek.

Grace was shocked that Jack dared to give such a mark to anyone. She knew he was a former rusher, but it was one thing to be told something and another to see the damage. She didn't care if the victim was a pirate.

Jack cleared his throat. "As I recall, Kay's man there challenged me to a duel and lost."

"Who knew a stable boy was so good with swords?" Kay cut Jack a strange, almost seductive look, and Grace suddenly felt a bit jealous of the woman. She hated how her eyes looked Jack over as if he were something to be conquered.

"Enough of that," Kay said. "Tell me, girl, who are you?"

"This is Grace Hilren, Kay," Ridley cut in. "The one I told

you about as we were walking."

"Ah yes, the noblewoman. You certainly are skinnier and shorter than I expected. I almost don't believe you could lift a sword, much less duel with one."

"I have had a bit of training. Besides, looking at you, I judge you are not nearly as frightful as tales would have us believe."

Kay glared hard at Grace and a great deal of tension formed between them. There was a silent battle raging, and neither looked like she would back down. Jack looked over at Ridley and shrugged.

"I can see you're no coward," Kay finally said. "Many a man has wet his trousers at a mere glance from me. I'm impressed; you have more gusto than I would have guessed."

"You have no idea." Grace rose from her seat; never taking her eyes off Kay. "But it's time I return to work. Those stalls aren't going to clean themselves."

Grace bowed her head in acknowledgment to Ridley and Jack. To Kay, she didn't even offer a goodbye. It was the sort of snub a noblewoman of Katherine's caliber would give.

Kay watched her go with great interest; thoroughly impressed with the girl's stubbornness. "She certainly has spirit."

"She's wonderful to have around, Kay," Ridley said cheerfully. "She has even been able to put up with Mayhew, and Jack has been less sharp and bitter toward everyone since Grace arrived."

"Has he?" Kay turned her eyes toward Jack and raised her eyebrow. Jack said nothing. He simply blew another smoke ring in Kay's direction.

~*~*~

After supper that evening, Grace and Ridley practiced knife fighting. The girl was still far better than Grace ever hoped to be, but she was catching up. That fact comforted her. Many of those she encountered as The Death Dealer were proficient enough with daggers and knives, so sword fighting was almost obsolete against them. The instruction received from Ridley was invaluable.

Not long into Ridley's lesson, Kay came down to join them. "Ridley, dear, mind stepping aside for me?" Kay removed her jacket and threw it aside. "I'd like to fight the noblewoman." Kay unsheathed her sword.

Ridley moved out of the way and one of Kay's men provided her with a sword; handing it to Grace.

"Not afraid are you, milady?" Kay mocked as she circled Grace.

"Afraid of a girl pretending to be a pirate? Hardly."

"Pretending?" Kay swung out with a high arc and Grace caught her blade with little effort. "Who's pretending?"

Kay tried a lower hit the second time around, but Grace caught her blade and smirked. She had no doubt Kay would try to pull something, so Grace stayed on her toes. Kay had a height advantage and more combat experience, she was sure, but Grace was faster and could read Kay's body movements even in the failing light. After so much time hunting bandits in the dark, her eyes became suited to fighting with little light for guidance. If Grace guessed correctly Kay had no formal training, which she hoped meant the pirate would be more uncoordinated.

"I've met kittens with more ferocity," Grace said.

In her anger Kay made for another high arc, which Grace sidestepped and blocked. Kay realized Grace would be able to block her shots all night and knew it was time to step things up a bit. Kay used her height and weight advantage and threw herself hard against Grace; catching Grace right where she wanted her. Grace brought her sword up to block Kay's downward arc and immediately knew the pirate planned to do something with Grace's midsection, since it was left wide open. Kay moved fast and caught Grace in the gut with her hilt. Grace felt winded and would have only staggered a little, but she let herself drop down to one knee. Grace kicked out hard and fast and her foot made contact with Kay's legs; knocking them out from underneath her. With a thud, Kay landed flat on her back. Grace jumped and hovered over her with her sword tip directly over her throat.

Kay was stunned at first, but slowly a smile crossed her face and she laughed. "Well done!" Grace held out her free hand and helped Kay to her feet. "Ridley, bring us some water!"

Ridley didn't need to be told twice. She hurried back to the Angel to fetch a bucket for the two women.

Kay wiped a bit of sweat off her face and clapped Grace on the back. "You're not as soft as you look. You used my own trick against me."

Grace was panting and nodded to Kay. "You have to be prepared for anything your opponent can throw at you, especially when they're bigger than you."

"I can see why Jack is so smitten with you." Grace was thrown off by Kay's remark, but the pirate only grinned. "Surely you could tell." Grace stared blankly at her. "Stupid girl. I've tried to win over Jack in the past, and you're barely here a season and you've already got him."

"I am sure you are mistaken."

Kay laughed under her breath. "I'm not stupid, noblewoman. I know a thing or two about Jack Anders." Kay looked down at Grace with fire in her eyes. She was jealous.

"Believe as you will," Grace replied, and returned the sword to Kay's man. She bowed to her opponent as a show of respect, but she was annoyed.

"You may be a decent swordswoman, but you can't even recognize attraction when you see it. So step aside and allow me to take over." She winked and gave Grace a condescending smirk.

"Whatever you think is happening, is not," was all Grace said on the subject.

~*~*~

That night, The Death Dealer took to the streets. The men of the *Fearless Dawn* were renowned throughout the city as scoundrels, and Grace needed to catch just one to make an example of him. The problem with this plan was that she might bring the wrath of the rest of the crew on herself. If she did manage to catch one of Kay's men, she hoped Marcus would be able to stop the pirate from any rash action.

A woman screamed nearby. Moving like a shadow through

the dark, Grace followed her ears to the source. The big man who sported Jack's scar was handling a young woman roughly. Grace could just see her angered face, and if she guessed correctly, this was one of Jim Little's barmaids. He would be most displeased to find out she was being mishandled.

"Scoundrel!" she cried as the man tried to get a firmer hold on her. "Let me go or I'll see to it 'ou get a whipping!" She slapped and punched at him.

"'Ou wouldn't do that to me." He laughed. The woman tried to get away but the pirate held her tightly. He barely flinched, even when she boxed his ear.

Grace unsheathed her sword and cleared her throat, and the pirate looked in her direction. He couldn't be sure who or what he was looking at, but he did recognize the reflection of steel in the streetlight. The woman seemed relieved. "The Death Dealer!" she cried out in joy; tears now visible on her rosy cheeks.

"Oye, so the stories be true. A fight 'ou looking for, sonny?" When the pirate threw the barmaid to the side, The Death Dealer didn't give him time to sufficiently react. Once his captive was freed, she made her move. He was distracted when the barmaid kicked his shin, and Grace used this to her advantage. Hurting him wasn't the plan tonight. Rather, Grace used the hilt of her sword to hit him upside the head; causing him to go down. His eyes remained open, so Grace gave him another good shot. This time he was knocked out.

The Death Dealer said, "Go back to the Angel and report this to Marcus." The woman ran off into the night and Grace set to work.

~*~*~

Kay fumed upon hearing of the attack on her man, Albert. Marcus's thieves found him bound and gagged in an alley about three blocks from the Angel Tavern. No one had ever challenged the men of the *Dawn* before, and Kay would be damned if someone dared to start now. Normally she could count on Marcus for aid, but apparently he knew Albert's attacker and seemed reluctant to help Kay track him down.

"Death Dealer? I fail to believe he just decided to help the Thieves' Guild out of the kindness of his heart," Kay spat out as she paced in front of Marcus's throne. "Not after killing whole bands of highwaymen before. I've heard stories of dozens of men dead on the road up north. He doesn't do favors for the likes of your people."

"The Death Dealer and I have an understanding. I leave him to his business and he leaves me to mine. Besides, your man accosted a barmaid. You can't seriously be thinking of letting him go?"

"I discipline my men, and Albert was duly punished by me for taking liberties, but it is *my* duty; not that of some upstart! Am I expected to sit back and let this dog harass my men?" Kay grabbed the arms of Marcus's throne. She was bent over, looking into his face carefully, with eyes blazing in fury.

"Don't act like your men are so guiltless, captain. Albert got what he deserved."

"I whipped him personally for his transgression, but he is my responsibility. I can't have people thinking I allow others to discipline my men! That I do not have a hold on my own crew."

"Take your hurt pride somewhere else, Kay. Albert is twice punished now and hopefully he's learned a lesson. That is what matters."

Kay's teeth were grinding in her skull, but she moved away from the throne. There'd be hell to pay if Kay ever caught The Death Dealer.

~*~*~

The Angel stayed relatively quiet the next day around the lunch hour, and Grace sat with Ridley as they ate their meals. They were enjoying the quiet and chatting softly to one another when the doors to the Angel swung open and an enraged Kay entered. She held out a small leather bag for all to see.

"Three pieces of gold for whoever brings me The Death Dealer!"

There was a long silence while Kay dangled the bag out for the patrons to see. Finally someone snickered from the corner, which only caused increased rage in the pirate. "What are you laughing at?" she growled; glaring menacingly at the crowd.

The laughter stopped and the culprit refused to say anything. With no one coming forward, Ridley stood. "Kay, while you strike fear into the hearts and minds of everyone who dwells in Glenbard, everyone here is more afraid of Marcus. And for one simple fact: he lives here always, while your arrivals are seldom in a year. Marcus formed an alliance with The Death Dealer, and if anyone takes that gold, they'll have to deal with him." Ridley laughed. "Three pieces is hardly enough to encourage anyone to cross the King of Thieves' new friend."

Grace watched the expression on Kay's face. It went from confused, to angry, to a look of utter annoyance. However, Ridley had obviously hit a chord with the pirate. The truth was that Kay was annoyed because on the *Dawn* she was in charge, but in Glenbard, Marcus was the King and she had no power. She might have influence over him, yet the final say was ultimately his. If Marcus liked The Death Dealer, her three pieces were useless. Kay realized this, and everyone in the inn saw the rage written plainly on her face.

"One day this Death Dealer will make a move against Marcus, and on that day my gold pieces will be available." And like she had burst in, she stormed out.

Ridley returned to her seat across from Grace. She resumed eating her food without so much as a word.

"Do you think she's right?" Grace finished her lunch and pushed her plate aside. "About The Death Dealer turning against Marcus?"

Ridley looked up from her fish and bread. "I suppose it's possible, but Marcus told me some things about the Death Dealer. I think if they betrayed one another, it would not be without just cause." So Ridley knew about the blood oath, and Grace now knew she had another supporter. Though the patrons of the Angel didn't take Kay's offer for fear of Marcus's punishment, that didn't mean others in the city wouldn't. Grace would have to be extra careful in the weeks to come.

~*~*~

That night, Grace entered the common room to find Kay and her pirates carousing. One of the *Dawn's* crewmen was playing a fiddle while his mates danced about or sang drunkenly with the barmaids and prostitutes. Only Kay seemed to be abstaining from the same sort of merrymaking as her fellows.

Instead, she was in Jack's corner occupying his attentions. And what a sight Kay was this evening. She had put away the hose and shirts and wore a fine silk dress that was dyed a rich red color. Her hair was down; a black, flowing wave over her shoulders and down her back. A finer lady in Glenbard Grace had not yet seen. Certainly in court women would be matched in beauty and grace, but here and now there was no equal to Kay. She easily held Jack's attention and pangs of jealousy ran through Grace, for she had no dresses that could rival the pirate captain. It was probably what Kay wanted Grace to feel. Her face flushed at the thought.

Looking about the room for a friendly face, her eyes fell upon Marcus. Unlike others who were making use of the common room, to the older man, Grace's entrance had not gone unnoticed. He crooked a finger and beckoned her toward him. Getting through the crowd of drunks and giggling women was no simple task, yet in the end she was rewarded with a seat at the King's table; an honor never before bestowed upon her.

Marcus had accepted Grace because Ridley did. He was happy to treat the girl with the same fatherly love as he did Ridley, but never before had he invited her to sit with him for any meal. Now Marcus dismissed the thieves that gathered around him. Even his man Thom left. Few were so blessed to enjoy a meal alone with the man.

"Your usual mates seem to be occupied this fine evening," he remarked, and turned his eyes toward Kay. Ridley joined them, though the pirate was far more interested in keeping Jack's attention. She was succeeding quite well, especially since Grace now saw how low-cut her dress was. It would have been a most immodest garment for her old life, yet it fit Kay's curvy form

129

well.

"She is quite beautiful tonight," Marcus continued. "Hardly a man can take his eyes off her. Not even Anders." As he planned, this got a stiff backed reaction from Grace. He laughed.

Suddenly Grace realized how jealous she really was and how embarrassing it was for her. After all, it was Jack. *Jack!*

"You're a young woman. You are allowed to wish to be the center of attention once in a while." His eyes gleamed in the candlelight of the inn's common room. "Vanity isn't always a curse. You must have seen this sort of thing at court. Perhaps there you played the role of Kay?"

Grace cleared her throat uncomfortably. "I was considered plain by many of the beauties."

"Fools." Marcus laughed again. He looked over at Kay as other locals came by to admire her beauty. They laughed at her jokes and she obviously enjoyed their compliments. "Kay is an intelligent woman, witty and fun. However, she's always felt she was the world's greatest living person. Even now she tempts my followers with gold to bring my death dealing friend to justice. Sometimes embarrassment serves to put one in her place."

"Sir?"

Kay finally looked in their direction. Seeing Grace, plain in her gray linen dress, she smirked. Had it been her plan all along to simply show her up? Marcus seemed to think so.

Marcus rose from his seat. "Court ladies are all well versed in dance, I assume?" Without waiting for an answer, he strode to the fiddler.

After a few quick words and the passing of a silver piece or two, the fiddler began a soft ballad. He signaled to Thom, who was engaging Jim in conversation. Thom broke away and moved to Kay's table. He asked for her hand and led her out to dance.

Marcus returned to Grace. "Watch." At first it was silly to sit and watch, but finally Grace understood what the King of Thieves had done. Kay stumbled and stepped on Thom's feet; much to her embarrassment and the room's amusement. Everyone howled in laughter. Kay's face turned a bright red and she stormed back to

Jack's corner.

Marcus took hold of Grace's hand and pulled her from her seat. Others came out to dance the ballad after Kay's failure, and now Marcus and Grace joined them. It was amazing to see that the thief was as good a dancer as he was. Certainly he hadn't been trained formally, but still his motions were fluid. With what Grace assumed was his natural skill and her training in such things, they were the best couple dancing. After the ballad ended, they returned to Marcus's usual table.

"That was unnecessary." Grace blushed, seeing that a few men were elbowing each other, pointing at her. Among them was a very surly-looking Mac. Kay had the same sort of sour expression on her face.

"You bested Kay with the sword I heard, but no one saw it. And here she comes in, attempting to look like a great court beauty, but she lacks the good manners to be one." Marcus reached across the table to pat Grace's cheek. "She comes here expecting royal treatment, and sometimes forgets her place in *my* city. Our little dance was for me to embarrass her for trying to get The Death Dealer's head, and also so you could show her you are not only a swordsman, but also a lady. Maybe some others took notice as well." He winked at her.

Marcus ordered food and took to chatting with Grace about her life before Glenbard. In the course of their meal, five men came forward to ask Grace for a dance, but she respectfully declined each one. She didn't want any more notice that night, so she just sat and enjoyed her chat with Marcus.

Around midnight, the Angel was almost cleared out. Jack was still in his corner and Kay had only just left his side. Grace got some tea and sat next to Jack.

"No activities tonight?" he asked; putting his feet up on the table.

"People in the Angel may not cross Marcus," she whispered, "but who knows who else heard about the gold?"

"A wise and safe choice. The first I've seen you make since your arrival."

131

"There is no need to treat me like that," she snapped with a glare.

"Don't ruffle your feathers, my little chick. I do not mean to hurt your pride so. Besides, you must be exhausted from turning down so many young men this evening. Would it be wise for you to run around all night? After all, belles of the ball need as much sleep as the rest of us." Jack smiled into his tankard and Grace realized he was toying with her.

"That was Marcus's doing. He was trying to make Kay look like a fool."

"While making you look better? Kay did come in here acting like a fine lady of the court. It was most certainly a change of character."

"She was quite beautiful tonight."

"In her own way. I wish she could have been beautiful away from me. Her perfume feels as though it will be forever burned into my nostrils. Besides, she halted my plans for the evening." Grace raised her eyebrows. "Five men looked to dance with you and each one met with defeat. I wanted to see if I could tempt you away from Marcus's company."

The two locked eyes. Grace read his face, looking for a hint of sarcasm or mockery. She found none, which was frightening. Thinking back to her jealousy from earlier in the evening and how Marcus pointed it out, she turned red under Jack's continued stare. Under normal circumstances this never would have happened.

"Get some sleep," he finally said. "You've more hearts to break tomorrow."

~*~*~

Kay and her men stayed for two more days and they did everything Jack said they would. The Death Dealer left the Guild alone, but she could not do the same for the crew of the *Fearless Dawn*. If she came across them at night being too friendly with someone who didn't want them to be, or if they were trying to steal from where they shouldn't, Grace came along and gave them a good whack on the back of the head with the hilt of her sword.

She refused to kill or seriously hurt any crew members, but she didn't mind giving them a bump they wouldn't soon forget.

Kay announced that she and her men would be leaving until winter passed. "It's warm here in Cesernan, but there's many merchant ships going in and out of Nareroc for the winter to escape the snow and cold of their own countries. It's every pirate's dream to plunder that many ships in a single season. But I'll be back, come the springtime."

Grace was glad to see Kay leave. The threat of the three pieces of gold would lessen because of her absence.

Ten

It had been three days since the men of the *Fearless Dawn* left and life was slowly returning to normal. Glenbard had been somewhat displaced during Kay's stay. Vendors in the market, fishermen at the dock, and patrons at the inns all had to change their routines as the crew passed through the lower city drinking, gambling, and trying to cheat people where they could. Even Jack, the great corner dweller of the Angel, had holed up in his room except during meals.

But now the pirates were gone and Grace was glad to return to looking after Mac. In the days the *Dawn* crew was ashore, she stopped watching the thief. Too many pirates were making too much noise around to keep an eye on the silent one. Now there was no telling what sort of plans he had made while Grace's back was turned.

For the past two nights, Grace had taken to the streets tailing Mac. He hadn't given her anything yet, but she knew he was up to something. No one kills an innocent girl related to Marcus without a plan. The whole mess provided a great headache across Glenbard's lower city. The Death Dealer and the Thief King were both becoming increasingly frustrated with the way things were going. Mac had to slip up eventually, but he was taking his sweet time.

Grace decided to give the hunt a rest for one night. Certainly one night without the hood wouldn't hurt anything. Instead, the night would be spent praying for guidance and paying a visit to Diggery's temple. The festival to the sun would be starting soon, which meant everyone would be celebrating Ciro and neglecting Kamaria's and Diggery's temples. Kamaria would have her own festival in the winter, but Diggery was not a celebrated god like the Divine Twins. To show her appreciation for the goddess of lost paths and wayward souls, Grace decided to take a night off from tracking Mac to prepare Diggery's temple. She hoped that by becoming a follower of the wolf, she would be able to find the correct path to reach Mac and stop him.

Grace brought some flowers to replace the wreath someone had placed around the wolf statue's neck. The old flowers were withered and crumbling onto the floor, while the new wreath added some color to the large black wolf. An elderly woman was also adding flowers and many colored ribbons to the temple.

"I prayed to Diggery when my lover left me alone with child." The old woman smiled at Grace. "She led me to the man who made me his wife. And he was kinder to me; never once raised his fists. I have the wolf lady to thank for that."

Grace stepped back to admire her work of the wolf statue and the old woman appeared by her side again. She was bent with age, but Grace could tell in this woman's youth she was tall and sturdy. Even now she was taller and stronger built than Grace.

"I come here once a week to give an offering to Diggery." The old woman sighed contentedly.

"It is good to know she is not neglected."

"Hardly. She is the patron here in Glenbard. Though I suppose up north you are not so acquainted with her." Grace raised an eyebrow. "The cook at the Angel gets his apples from my stand in the marketplace. He said the disgraced noblewoman was mucking out stables for Jim Little, and he's pointed you out a few times when I drop off his apples. I suppose you come here so Diggery might change your luck and lead you away from the muck and scum of this poorest of areas."

Grace rarely found herself far from the Angel Inn. The inn was set up near the poorest district of Glenbard, since most of the patrons were under the Thieves' Guild's protection and those were the poorer classes. Grace was aware of the dirty, crowded streets of the poor districts; the urine and vomit and blood that worked its way through the night daily. She heard tell of the crying, hungry children and screams from drunken fathers. The Angel was safe and comforting, but outside was cruel and unforgiving. As Grace Hilren, she chose not to venture forth from her home over the stables. As The Death Dealer, she walked those disregarded streets nightly.

"Don't look offended, dearie. No shame in wishin' for

135

wealth. I suppose spending time with horses is as dirty as you would like to get."

If only this old woman knew that as The Death Dealer Grace went into those dark corners of Glenbard, doing what the King's guard didn't. She figured it was safer not to know the people she helped. Then they couldn't betray her.

Grace smiled and picked up her empty basket that had held her flowers; placing it in the crook of her arm. "I am content here, Mother. It is a new and exciting life for me."

The old woman took both of Grace's hands in hers. "Then may the Lady Diggery keep you on the path that makes you happiest. It warms my heart to see a new face in her temple."

Grace took her hands back and produced a piece of silver. "Next time you bring apples to the Angel, bring me some and we shall speak of Diggery some more."

Taking her leave from the temple, Grace headed into the night. It was just as warm in the night as it had been during the day when the sun beat down. There was no breeze in the summer months, not even from the sea. Instead the air in Glenbard just became stagnant. According to Ridley, this was not uncommon for summer in the city. This sort of weather caused a great deal of longing for Arganis, but Grace would survive.

The Angel was about four blocks from the temple district. At night the walk could be treacherous, but it was still fairly early. It would be a few hours before the worst would crawl from their hiding places to cause misery. This early, even Marcus wasn't sending his thieves out. So Grace walked home, swinging her basket, not worrying about the danger that was out there.

Out of the shadows two men jumped, although they weren't as coordinated as they should have been. One moved seconds before the other, alerting Grace of his presence. She didn't have time to run, but she did have time to drop her basket and grab her dagger from within the folds of her dress. Knowing they were spotted, the men blocked her path; one before her and one behind.

"Lassie, best put down that little knifey," the one in front said. "We just want to talk, and if you hurt one of us, we gonna have to send more out."

Normal ruffians didn't bother with pleasantries. They generally attacked and left. "What do you want?"

"Our boss don't like being challenged, especially by a woman." Grace's mind flashed to Mac. So he *did* have more support, just like Marcus suspected. Did he know about her secret?

The one behind her spoke now, saying, "Follow us nicely, so our boss can show you how women need to act." She could feel the one behind her advancing, though the man in front stood still.

The next few seconds passed in a blur and Grace wasn't thinking clearly. Then she did something she knew she shouldn't do: she screamed for help, threw the dagger at the man in front of her, and ran as he tried to dodge it. It was a foolish move to throw her only weapon, but the shock of the throw gave her just enough time to get past the man before her as the second jumped and missed her by a hair. She took off away from the men, hoping they wouldn't be fast enough to catch her. If they were able to get her, she wouldn't have anything to defend herself with. She cursed her stupidity as she ran along the street.

For a few blocks she heard sounds of pursuit, but they faded as she drew toward the light of the Angel. She burst through the door and all eyes turned toward her. Marcus sat in his throne with Ridley at his side. Mac was nowhere to be seen.

The King of Thieves beckoned to her. He led her into a private room he only used for the most secret of affairs, and wouldn't even let Ridley follow. He had Grace tell the tale of her frantic entrance into the inn. "Mac's been absent from my halls lately. No doubt cookin' up trouble. Do you guess the same, dear?"

Grace nodded. Marcus called for a serving wench to bring some ale for Grace. Her hands shook, but she drank it anyway. Marcus sat her down in a chair at the long table he used for conferences of the Thieves' Guild. He sat next to her, watching her face carefully.

"He has the temper of a rabid dog. I can't tell what he's up to, but I have plans in place. However, it's harder to get a hold of him than I thought." Marcus paused. "This is the second time he has harassed you. He hates loose ends, and he's goin' to make you suffer before unleashin' whatever he has planned. You've vexed him by simply working in the stable that houses that beast of his. He punishes people who annoy him, even over the slightest offense. Tomorrow I'm putting you on one of my horses and setting you on the road for a while. It'll get you out of harm's way and maybe Mac will make a move without you as a loose end around here. Right now he's being sneaky and slippery. He knows most of my secrets, and that makes him more deadly than my other enemies."

"Marcus, is this really the best course of action?"

"It might not be, but you *will* leave this city for a safer location."

"Why are you helping me? I'm not a loyal thief or a family member."

Marcus cocked an eyebrow in her direction. "Because I'm no oath breaker."

Thousands of thoughts swirled in Grace's head in the blink of an eye. Did he truly know, or was he guessing and trying to force her to confirm? She was so careful! How could he have guessed?

Marcus smiled as he watched her think. She tried to keep her face like stone, although she wondered if she was succeeding. "That is a matter we will not speak of again, including how I learned it was you. Though let me say this: you aren't strong enough for such a foe. Not yet, and you may never be. The Guild will handle Mac, and you will leave Glenbard for a time."

"But for how long? And how will I know when to return? What of Mayhew and my job?"

"Send me a letter to let me know you're safe. Instead of saying outright where you are, leave subtle hints as to your location so if the letter falls into the wrong hands, they might not guess. I will speak with Mayhew. He is not so hard as to turn a deaf ear to his king." Marcus rose and patted Grace's shoulder. "A horse will be waiting in a stall before sunrise tomorrow. Be gone before the sun is up."

~*~*~

In her room, Ridley and Jack were waiting. With Donald gone, it was nice to know there were others looking out for her. Grace sat on her bed, Ridley sat next to her and Jack leaned against the door.

"Your face," Ridley said. "You're paler than you was when you came in. What did Marcus say? What happened?"

"Men attacked me in an alley and Marcus has some ideas as to who ordered it." She couldn't be sure how much Ridley knew, but she felt it was safer to let her friends come to their own conclusions.

"That beast has been pretty absent lately," Jack said. "Haven't seen him around much since Kay arrived."

"Then it was Mac? What did Marcus say? Why do you look more terrified than when you came in?" Grace couldn't explain to Ridley about how Marcus guessed she was The Death Dealer.

"He insisted I leave Glenbard for a bit, at least until something is done."

"Send you away? Madness!" Ridley crossed her arms over her chest. "What good is sending you away gonna do? You're safer here with us."

"Clearly, since she can't even come home from the temple district without an escort. Marcus is doing the right thing."

The Princess of Thieves huffed and grumbled. "That was just bad luck. We can keep an eye on her here. On the road there's no protection."

"There is if she has someone to turn to, and no doubt Marcus has a plan – one to be kept secret since there's no telling where there are spies. Now, you silly girl, get Grace something to eat."

Ridley left the room in a huff and Jack moved out of the way; letting her slam the door in her fit. The anger lingered for a moment in her absence. "She doesn't want to lose a friend."

"This is folly. I should stay here. Marcus could use me as bait to draw Mac out."

"Is he going to have to crack your skull and break every bone

139

in your body before you realize Mac is too strong for you? Don't be stupid."

Grace knew she was weak against Mac, but she didn't like being reminded or being told she was stupid.

"Don't tell me I am stupid!"

"Then stop being so foolish!" Jack's voice was getting louder, so he closed his eyes and took a deep breath. When he composed himself, he looked carefully at Grace.

Grace retorted, "I am trying to help Marcus. You wouldn't understand that sort of loyalty. Go back to your table and climb into your pint like you always do."

Jack threw his hands in the air. His composure didn't last long. "I will *not* take advice from a girl who has disgraced herself and who will put herself in danger to draw out a murderer and a thief – *all* for her own foolish stubbornness."

"And why should *I* listen to a former stable boy who does nothing but hide from everyone? No doubt you were removed from King Frederick's stables due to your uselessness and hatred."

"Don't *ever* speak to me about my former life, you stupid harlot! In fact, stay here and get yourself killed – *then* see who mourns you!" Like Ridley, Jack stormed out. Only when he slammed the door, it was with enough force to shake her tiny room.

Grace lay down on her bed and ignored the door when Ridley returned. She only called out that she needed to sleep.

~*~*~

In the morning, Mayhew informed Grace that Marcus had left her a roan colored mare named Olwen. He also told her Marcus's right hand man, Thom, would escort her for three days to wherever they thought was safe. The old stable master was angry, but a few threats from Marcus eased his tongue somewhat. With Thom by her side, Grace took the southern road from Glenbard and didn't look back toward the city. Her pride still hurt from Jack's words and from the fact Marcus didn't want her around to help him.

Eleven

Grace,

I admire your courage and fortitude. It is rare to see a heart that beats with the bravery yours does. Though King Frederick and many others wish to punish such daring, I think it should be rewarded. You beat a prince in the sword ring and you did it fairly. Do not think for a moment that I believe those silly claims of witchcraft. I have no doubts your cousin made sure you know you are welcomed in Arganis, but allow me to extend my home to you as well. The barony of Egona is ever open to you, regardless of your title or place in this world.

Your friend and ally in these troubled times,
Henry

On her first night on the road, Grace read Henry's letter from the day she was sent into exile. She then resolved to make for his castle in Egona, which was a four-day journey from the city of Glenbard. Thom did as promised and rode with her for the first three days to make sure no danger followed them outside of Glenbard.

Now here she was. The path she was on led straight to Henry's grounds. The sun was beginning to set, and at the steady walking pace Olwen was moving, Grace wouldn't make it before the sun went down and the gates were closed for the night.

"Come on, girl. You know you want warm mash tonight, and I would rather not sleep on a tree root." Grace gently kicked Olwen's sides and the horse began to trot. Grace nudged her on into a canter and then finally into a gallop.

The two flew through the gates and Grace pulled her horse to a stop. Olwen panted underneath her and Grace patted her lovingly on the neck. A servant from the stables came out and eyed Grace with suspicion.

"Who are you?"

"My name is Grace. I have come to see Lord Henry."

The servant looked over Grace and her attire. She was

dressed in the travel-stained breeches she had worn on her journey from Frederick's castle in Ursana. "I will see if the master of this house is with anyone at present."

Grace was left alone in the courtyard. She slipped off of Olwen and dug for a lump of sugar in her pockets. Olwen gladly accepted it and nibbled at Grace's pockets, looking for more. The sun was failing fast. Finally, the doors to the castle opened and the portly figure of Henry emerged.

He moved as fast as he could and lifted Grace up into a great hug. "What a wonderful surprise!"

"Henry, it is so wonderful to see you again!"

"Someone take the lady's horse and stable it."

A stable boy, barely thirteen years of age, rushed from the stables and took Olwen by the reins. He bowed to Grace and Henry. "Yes, my lord."

"Oh, I can take care of my horse myself, Henry."

"Nonsense. You are a guest in this house and you will be treated as such. Now, you must be tired and hungry. I shall see what supper is available to you, and then I will have a bath drawn."

"And it will be off to bed with me, I am afraid."

"As you wish, Grace. We here at Egona will make you welcome and comfortable."

~*~*~

The next morning Grace wrote a lengthy letter to Calvin and Cassandra, and one of Henry's messengers was sent to Arganis to deliver it. Then she composed one for Ridley and Marcus, letting them know she went to Egona and was staying with the count there. As instructed, she did not say outright where she was, though she guessed Thom would tell them.

She learned a great deal from Henry about the tournament after she left. Calvin was offered the chance to enter the sword ring against Prince Drake, but due to his injury he forfeited and withdrew from the rest of the tournament. Many gossiped about Grace after the incident, and Calvin, Henry, and even Drake were her main defenders. No one could ever get Drake to say why he supported her, but most believed Grace practiced witchcraft and had beguiled him. Tristan spoke out against her the most, and it still hurt a great deal when Grace heard it. Hypocrisy, feigned love and infatuation were things she did not enjoy.

Grace told Henry she had been holed up in Glenbard working as a stable girl, but she avoided telling him why she felt the need to run off from that life. She simply said she left unexpectedly to get away and Henry never pried. He figured she would tell him when she was ready. She gladly told him about Ridley, but she left out the 'Princess of Thieves' title.

Over a week passed and Grace had plenty of time to grieve; both over her lost life at court, as well as her lost friends such as Calvin and Cassandra. Upon entering Glenbard, she found herself too busy to really think of her loss, although of course she still found time to feel horrible about what happened between herself and Tristan. She also thought about how she was forced out of Glenbard for her safety and realized she was somewhat relieved to be gone. That had to do with Jack as well as the threat from Mac. She wanted to confront Mac again, but she wanted to beat him the next time. She couldn't beat him if every few days she encountered him and never had a chance to improve her skills. And Jack…well, Jack simply hurt her pride by thinking she was incapable of anything because she had once been a member of the King's court. She hoped she'd never have to face Jack again. He was just one big pain in her side.

The week of Grace's arrival the weather was fair. Henry took her out riding and hunting, and even showed her some sword and knife play she could use to protect herself. But at the start of her second week with Henry, the rain came down in buckets and lightning streaked across the sky. Grace felt gloomy and the weight of all her mistakes of the last few months pressed down on her. Her mood felt much like the weather outside. Henry was sitting across from her, eating breakfast and being his usual jovial self, when Grace felt compelled to ask him a question.

"Are you content with your life here, Henry?" she blurted out between one of her bites of porridge.

Henry was startled by Grace's question. She always avoided talking about her own life's contentment and stuck to facts when she told Henry about how she was faring these days. To Henry's credit, he knew she just wasn't ready to say how she really felt.

"Content? I daresay I am. I have seen wars and I have been a knight for many long years. I have sailed to different countries and fought to protect this land. I was lucky enough to be married to a wonderful woman, and though my dear wife has passed on, I am happy to have married and loved her for so long. I would say that qualifies as contentment." Grace nodded and forced a weak smile. "The question is, are you?"

"I am not sure these days. I was happy for a while in Glenbard, but it was short-lived. A few of the people there hate me now that they know I am a noble in exile, and they wish to see my head on a pike as a warning to other nobles who dare to hang around with commoners like they belong. And there are people who constantly cause me trouble, even when they are trying to help. It can be such a dangerous and unforgiving place."

"I see, but it will pass, Grace. If you like living in Glenbard, you should return some day. I would love for you to stay here with me, but I don't think that is what you want."

"Henry, you have been a good friend to me despite everything, and although I wish I could stay, I know one day before long I should head back. I am not sure how my return is going to be taken. I was driven out for a time because of..." she thought for a moment, "unpleasantries. I wonder how long I can survive in such a place."

"It sounds like Marcus, Ridley and Jim would like to see you come back and would keep you from harm."

"But there is someone else, and I don't think he will be so happy. He alone provides plenty of reasons for me not to return. He is a bitter, resentful man who used to be a stable boy for King Frederick. Perhaps you know him? He says he was the best one the King ever had, though somehow I doubt it." Henry raised an eyebrow and waited for Grace to give him a name. "Do you know Jack Anders?"

Any sign of a smile washed away from Henry's face. He stared at Grace with his mouth gaping open like a newly caught fish. "You said Jack Anders?" Grace nodded slowly, not sure what the name could possibly mean to Henry. He was a lord, while Jack was merely a stable boy. "He told you he was the King's best stable boy?"

"He said he was the best thing that ever happened to the court."

"Jack certainly wasn't lying about that. But he really told you he was a stable boy? Oh, Jack." Henry shook his head and groaned a little.

"He wasn't a stable boy, then?"

"Jack was no stable boy, though I am not surprised that he lied to you or that you could not tell who he really was. He is nothing like his father or his brother, but I had no idea he was still around Glenbard. I would have gone to see him if I had known." Henry was now talking more to himself than Grace.

"Henry?"

"Grace, Jack Anders is Tristan of Escion's older brother."

~*~*~

As summer moved along, the people across Cesernan gathered in the temples of Ciro to bid the Sun King to continue his good fortune and not speed winter along. A week-long festival was held in his honor, and now the last day of the festival drew to a close.

Ridley sat next to Marcus in the temple of Ciro and listened to the priest drone on. She could not have cared less; she was only thinking of what to say to Jack, who was seated in front of her.

The Princess of Thieves was still angry at Jack for making Grace cross before she left. Whenever Jack was in earshot she bemoaned that Grace was the only girl close to her age to hang around the Angel in many years, and now she was gone. Jack just ignored her whining.

"You should be ashamed of yourself," Ridley hissed in Jack's ear.

He turned his head a bit so she could catch his profile, and then he rolled his eyes. "Will you let it die already? Grace is gone and you harping on me is not going to bring her back."

"You could go to Egona and apologize. You know where she's at; her note implied as much. You were a stable boy for the King! Surely you know this Henry fellow and can get in to see Grace."

"You want me to ride to Egona and apologize? You want me to take the time and energy to go there? Certainly you can wait until Marcus deems it safe for her to come back."

The sun priest finished speaking for the day and dismissed those in attendance; bidding them to be careful at the festival. The people herded themselves out to fill their bellies with festival food and enjoy the crooked games the traveling merchants set up. Ridley moved fast to leave Jack's presence, but Marcus made sure to get close to him. Marcus's man, Thom, hung back a few steps as the men moved out into the streets.

No merchants were allowed to peddle their goods in the temple district, but they could be heard all the way from the marketplace. Some merchants were able to survive for a whole year on the profits they made during the festival to Ciro, so they called loudly and frequently to passersby.

"Marcus..." Jack started. He thought the King of Thieves would have spoken before now, but he did not. "How fares the lower city today?"

"Don't play the fool, Master Anders. You know I sent Grace away in hopes of moving my man out of hiding. But he is cool and calculating when he needs to be, and it seems he will just sit back and wait now."

"Majesty?"

"He's not going to be drawn out because our girl is gone. Perhaps I can trust you and Ridley to retrieve Grace from her hiding place?"

"It is quite possible, but why give a care for a stable girl like Grace? She'll not make a fine wife for your thieves. She's on the straight path."

"Kings before me have done some wicked things, but I'm not

146

a man to break my oaths. And vigilantes come in all sizes, even little stable girl sizes. I could use the extra set of eyes." Marcus picked up his pace and became lost in the throngs of people with Thom close behind.

Jack stepped off to the side and into an alley. Not only did Marcus know about Grace's secret, but he had somehow guessed Jack knew it too. Jack rubbed his temples. This gave him a headache he didn't need, but it did explain Marcus's interest in keeping Grace safe. He swore a blood oath to The Death Dealer and it fell on him to keep her safe, whether in her executioner garb or not.

But how much did Marcus know? If he was able to sort through Mac's lies then he would be able to guess the scoundrel killed his cousin, yet he didn't make a move against him. That was puzzling. The depths of the King's knowledge couldn't be guessed, and Jack wondered if there was more to Mac and his plans than Marcus wished to let on. He couldn't be certain of his allies, not when Mac was sending rushers of his own out to harm friends of the Guild.

Now he was recalling Grace back to Glenbard. Either he thought Mac was more interested in something else or he wanted her return to be widely known so Mac would move quickly. Jack couldn't be sure, since he had no knowledge of Mac or the patterns of his thinking. Marcus said that although he was calculating, he could lose patience. Was Marcus going to dangle Grace – a frustration of Mac's – before him to draw him out? Jack disliked the idea that she could be hurt in a game of thieves. Still, he wasn't about to contend with Marcus. The King wouldn't bring harm to his friends if he thought he could fail, and there was no telling what Marcus would do if Jack tried to cross him.

~*~*~

Grace sat by the fire while Henry paced around his study. The two had moved from the dining room to the study to avoid any interruptions from the servants. Grace fidgeted in her seat, anxious to hear what Henry had to say.

"His birth name is Jonathan Mullery of Escion, but we all

147

called him Jack. He was King Frederick's best knight. Even Benjamin of Salatia could not best him in the practice ring, although they never formally competed in tournament. Jack never saw a tournament after gaining his shield, but I assure you Jack would have been the champion. And he was nothing like his father or brother, whom you have already met. Tristan's father is too much like Frederick in that he refuses to compromise and follows anything the King says, even if it is folly. Courage, like that which you showed, foolish though it was, was still worthy of note." Henry gently patted Grace's hand as he said this, to soften his message. "But as I was saying, the man keeps several mistresses and his poor wife lives in misery. Tristan follows closely in his footsteps, and it grieved me to know that he had set his sights on you.

"But Jack – Jack was far nobler than that. He was the apple of his mother's eye, and he felt women had more of a place in the world than simply bearing children. He looked for an intelligent woman who could educate their children and not just bear them. How he loved and respected his mother. She was a loving and brilliant woman who deserved better than her lot in life. I was glad to know Prince Drake looked up to Jack, and there is still hope that Drake will not turn out like his father and Jack will be able to return to court if he wishes it. However, Jack was cast out in disgrace. No one even speaks of him anymore, unless it is behind closed doors and far from certain ears."

The name of Jonathan Mullery was not completely unknown to Grace. She had heard Calvin speak it in whispers to her uncles, but until now it was just a mysterious name that heralded bad things. "What happened to him? Why was he cast out?"

"The Lady Danielle of Sera; a snake disguised as a lady. Jack fell in love as soon as he laid eyes on her. When Jack was about seventeen, still naïve in the ways of love and the world, she came from Sera with many lords to celebrate the fiftieth birthday of His Majesty. It was to be a celebration of good faith between our kingdoms. Jack did everything to win her heart and she barely glanced his way…until she found some wicked use for him and his willing heart.

"Danielle longed for a very precious piece of jewelry that was owned by Katherine of Actis. An heirloom of Katherine's house, a beautiful emerald pendant that was the envy of most women in court, she treasured it. Danielle begged Jack to steal it for her, along with much of Katherine's allowance from Actis, and then she promised they could run away together. The gold would ensure their passage to the Nareroc Islands and give them a great life there. Or so she told Jack. Blinded by his love, Jack did the unthinkable. He stole from Katherine and presented the jewels and gold to Danielle.

"She took them but refused to run; saying Jack was 'just a silly boy.' He was hurt and confused by her actions and begged her to keep her promise, proclaiming his love and telling her it would kill him if she did not marry him. But Danielle refused. Jack shook her by her shoulders and continued to beg, however she just sent him away and took the stolen gifts for herself.

"Later that night, the guards came to arrest poor Jack. Danielle claimed he stole the jewelry and tried to buy her with it, and when that failed he threatened her life, even striking her. Other lords have taken poor peasant girls, but the fact one had gone after a noblewoman was appalling. Those from Sera demanded Jack be beaten, and some even suggested execution, but Frederick hated to waste Jack's life, knowing how good he was in battle. If our country were to go to war, a soldier like Jack would be very valuable. It would be a waste to destroy a man like that. The King also knew Sera was just looking for an excuse to strain their relationship further.

"So I spoke on Jack's behalf and begged the people to listen to reason. I knew Jack would never commit such crimes and many others did too, but no one spoke up. Danielle spoke, saying that though there was an attempt against her virtue, Jack did not succeed and she was relatively unscathed. Jack did not even bother to defend himself. Eventually Prince Drake came forward. He said he witnessed everything that transpired, and that Jack shook Danielle for her treachery and screamed at her, but did nothing else, rather he stormed off to lick his wounds. Following the courage of His Highness, the lady's maid also came forward, saying she was instructed to lie on Lady Danielle's behalf. Finally Frederick released Jack from the court and stripped him of his inheritance and claim to Escion. The act was to assuage the delegates from Sera, because his own father would not have cared if he had been killed.

"Jack begged to be executed, saying he could not live in such a world as this. But Frederick felt it was more of a punishment to send him away. Jack's mother tried to stay in contact with him, as did I. We would sometimes go in disguise to see him in Glenbard or wherever he was. That was all of seven years ago, and we have not heard from him for over two years now. I was beginning to think he left Cesernan altogether. I must send word to his mother. It will warm her heart to know her eldest son is alive."

Grace hung her head in shame. She judged Jack so harshly, and he had already suffered far more than she. Luckily her infatuation with Tristan didn't lead her down the same twisted, dark path Jack's love of Danielle brought him. Henry let her sit in silence for a few minutes; guessing her thoughts and hoping she would not be too hard on herself.

"I should return to Glenbard and make amends."

"I hope you stay a while longer here. I enjoy your company and would hate to lose the companionship you have brought here. Besides, isn't your friend going to send someone to fetch you when he deems it safe? Don't rush back just yet, my dear."

Henry smiled warmly at her. Grace knew he had been kind to her, letting her stay with him even though if any from court found out, he would be disgraced for sure. But she did feel a longing for Glenbard. When she first arrived to Henry's, she didn't ever wish to return. Yet now she thought of how she judged Jack too harshly and how much she missed Ridley's carefree nature. She even missed old cranky Mayhew. Still, Marcus said he would retrieve her when the time was right. Best to stay where she was until then.

~*~*~

Grace awoke the next morning to find Henry gone. A servant informed her that while the master of the house left on an errand and would be gone some days, he requested Grace stay and wait for him to return. She wanted to return to Glenbard, but she had to thank Henry for his kindness first. She was going to have to find ways to keep herself busy until he returned.

She sat alone in Henry's great library, reading what she could. She had never cared much for reading or for any of her other studies, for that matter. Her Uncle George saw to it that she was well-educated, but nothing seemed to stick. However, being there in the library sitting amongst Henry's books from countries around the world, George would have been proud. As Grace pulled down a book from Archon, she began to understand why her uncle was so in love with the written word.

The histories and adventures written in the numerous scrolls and great leather-bound volumes provided a pleasant, momentary escape. They were nothing compared to life beyond their pages, yet she saw how it was possible for them to provide clarity and maybe even guidance. Spending hours among the books made Grace long for her Uncle George so he could continue to teach her. She might even pay attention this time.

From Archon, Grace read of a great battle that took place in the famed Ninia Valley. The battle took place before what was known as the Great Alliance was formed. In this valley between Sera and Archon, invaders from Sera fought across the northernmost reaches of Archon with a force of men that outnumbered Archon's by three to one. Sera's victory was expected to be swift, but a young prince from Archon refused to accept the defeat of his homeland and he *fought*. He fought like a man possessed, and the day was his. Sera was beaten back and Archon remained a sovereign nation.

This victory didn't seem so uncommon. From all Grace learned, Eurur had faced these odds before, as had some of the eastern kingdoms. Since history was often repeated, was it possible someone like The Death Dealer had existed years before Grace first donned her executioner's hood? Grace laid aside the book and thought this over. It was a heartening thought.

~*~*~

Henry was picking along the road to Glenbard. He had seen no one yet and sorely missed a friendly face and a nice chat, which just showed him how used to comfortable living he had become. He packed for a journey and saddled his horse well before sunrise, because he wanted to be off toward Glenbard before Grace woke. He needed to see Jack alone. Now as Henry took to the road, he wished he had remembered a bed roll. No doubt he would be spending a few lonely nights out under the stars with naught but a thin blanket.

Ahead of him, two riders were coming up the road. One of the riders stopped his horse and watched Henry. There was something familiar in the scene, but Henry couldn't quite place it. The horse and rider were too far away to make anything out. The second rider stopped and glanced back at his partner.

"Hello there, fellow traveler! Any news of the road ahead?"

The first rider laughed and began to trot his horse forward. "As I live and breathe, Lord Henry of Egona." The rider signaled for his partner to hang back.

"Jack Anders!" Jack stopped before Henry. "And Pilgrim, old boy."

Jack smiled at Henry.

"I see Pilgrim is well taken care of. He really was the King's finest. Too bad he did not show it as a colt. He would probably be Drake's horse by now if he hadn't been such a scrawny handful back then." Henry looked upon Jack and saw the same knight he knew so many years ago. Such honor and renown suited Jack. "I am happy to see you, boy. What brings you on this road?"

"I think you know."

"I am surprised. Ever since leaving us at court, you haven't been one to go trying to make amends with anyone. What makes you come this time?"

"Who said anything about trying to make amends?"

"You don't fool me, Jack."

Jack shrugged. "I think this time an apology is in order. I've been wrong every step of the way with Grace, and my friend sent me along with his adopted daughter to retrieve her."

"It is not entirely your fault. You were hurt by a woman of the court, but not all women are like Lady Danielle. Grace certainly isn't."

"She really isn't like anyone, man or woman, that I've ever met. Fighting as a knight – now *there's* a step of idiocy, but it does take skill. And to think that if Daniel were still alive, she would never even know how to handle a sword."

"Don't speak of that to her. She remembers her father as a noble man, not a close-minded brute. I know better than anyone that Grace's father would never have let her learn to use a weapon, even if her life depended on the ability to protect herself. He would rather have her killed than wield a sword. I am thankful Sir Leon had more sense than his older brother and made sure Grace could defend herself. It is best to let her keep the memory of her father intact."

"Perhaps." Jack fell silent. His face clouded with memories and thoughts Henry could only guess at.

"It is all in the past, Jack. I know you have wished for death these past few years, but life is still worth living."

"I don't wish to die anymore, Henry." Jack stroked Pilgrim's neck as the horse fidgeted beneath him.

"Is that so?"

"I never thought I would have a reason to live after Danielle, but I think I've found one now."

"It would ease my heart if that were true, but come. Your reason is not far away. If we ride hard and fast, we can make it before sundown. And call your friend...she is fidgeting back there."

Jack waved Ridley forward and Henry bowed in his saddle to her. "Young lady, you must be Ridley Hunewn of Glenbard. I have heard a good deal about you, but Grace's stories have spoken nothing of your beauty."

Ridley smiled. "My lord, you needn't try to flatter a poor commoner like me. I'm just happy to be let into your home."

Thusly introduced, the three turned their horses toward Henry's home.

Twelve

When Grace woke the next morning, the servants in the kitchen told her that Henry returned late the night before and was still asleep. Grace was happy to hear the news. She looked forward to talking to him and finding out where he had gone, though she had a pretty good idea.

Grace grabbed an apple for breakfast and headed out to take Olwen for a quick ride around the grounds. It would be a few hours before Henry woke, and she had plenty of time to continue exploring the area around his castle.

As she was brushing Olwen, another horse neighed and stamped his hoof. Grace followed the noise and was shocked to see Pilgrim shaking his head back and forth, trying to get her attention. The gelding was excited to see her.

"Pilgrim? But how is this possible?"

"Don't dwell on how this is a possibility, Grace."

Grace swung around and saw Jack feeding a sugar cube to Olwen. "Jack!" She hated his ability to move about with catlike silence, but this didn't dampen her sudden happiness at seeing him. She rushed forward and threw her arms around him for a big hug. Grace could tell Jack was caught off-guard and didn't know quite how to respond to it. He probably expected her to still be sore with him after fighting over her battle with Mac.

"Hey now, no need for that." Jack pushed Grace a little ways back.

"Oh, Jack, I am so sorry." Grace wanted to hug him again, but when she tried he put his arm up to block her. "I judged you so horribly from the start and I didn't even know what hardships had fallen on you. I understand it now, and I understand why you were so beastly toward me."

He shook his head. "You can't really understand it, Grace, and you shouldn't be apologizing. No one knows at the Angel, and I like it that way. I'd rather have them think of me as a bitter stable boy than a disgraced knight. Yet you and I share a common background. I should have explained this to you when you first arrived. Before learning each other's secrets, we were enemies when we should have been allies. Even bitter men such as me get lonely and long for a companion from time to time."

"Oh, Jack!" After hearing of his past, the young woman spent a great deal of time thinking about the cards life had dealt her and her friends. "It is so unfair. To think no one would believe you except Henry."

"And Drake and a fair number of others, but they were foolish to put so much faith in me. I didn't act as a knight should, and for that I am duly punished. I am ashamed of myself for my past. I didn't steal anything and I didn't force myself on anyone, but I wasn't kind to Danielle either. The verbal barbs I threw at you when you arrived? I did the same to her, only worse. I screamed and berated her. It was wrong, but I could not stop myself." He sighed. "However, you'll notice Henry has great faith in those who are accursed and cast out. I understand he had a bit of faith in you as well."

Grace smiled and nodded in agreement. "So here we are, two outcasts. Both befriended by the only member of court who seems to care about someone other than himself."

"And of course we are both honorary members of the Thieves Guild. I do hope you'll come back to see the Guild with me. Ridley has been an absolute terror since you left. Her constant nagging is part of the reason I was sent in search of you. When she wakes up I'm sure she will chatter on until you are deaf. Marcus wants you to return as well. I believe he has some scheme worked out for you. If I've guessed correctly, he's grown tired of Mac's hiding and thinks you may help fuel the fool's anger."

"Are those the only reasons? Marcus could easily have sent Thom and Ridley. I know how you dislike being removed from your corner."

He smiled and patted Grace's shoulder and said, "We're friends, aren't we? And friends try to make amends after arguments."

"You consider me a friend?"

"You are stubborn and a pain to me, but you have trusted me

with your secrets and now I trust you with mine." This was the first time Jack had smiled at her beyond a cruel smirk. All his teeth showed in this genuine display. Grace liked it. It brought an equally large smile to her face.

"And you are a brute and far too mean to others, but I know I am safe with you around. I guess we are friends, Jack. That makes me happy."

"So you'll return to Glenbard with me? The King of Thieves commands it of you."

"Of course. I should be returning soon anyway. Donald will be coming back from Nareroc soon and I miss the Angel dreadfully."

Jack dared to reach out and touch Grace's face. The two locked eyes; Grace's heart pounded against her ribcage. Since leaving Ursana in disgrace and the way Tristan treated her, she believed no one would ever look on her as Jack now did. The pain of love crossed Grace's face...*Tristan and Danielle*...and the past clouded her mind.

Jack's hand dropped away. "No need to think on those things." He patted her shoulder again and kissed her forehead tenderly before offering her his arm. "Let's go wake up Ridley."

~*~*~

Ridley bit into an apple and openly admired Henry's library. "There is so much here! Do you mean to tell me that Henry read all these?" The thought that someone could read so much was almost beyond Ridley's comprehension. She could barely write her own name, and yet here was a vast collection only one man had read.

"My Uncle George has a library that rivals this," Grace said. She spent the entire morning occupying Ridley while Henry and Jack talked. The moment in the stables weighed on her mind. Grace felt giddy. She wanted to tell Ridley, but the girl's chatter about Henry's home blocked out anything Grace wanted to say.

"Is this what nobles do? People in Glenbard bathe in filth and fight like wet cats to scratch a livin', and here you sit before fires readin' this nonsense." Though Ridley's words were bitter, the

157

girl's tone was filled with humor. "Not a life I'd mind livin'. Is Henry looking for a wife, by any chance?"

"If you married Henry, who would keep Marcus in line?"

"You just don't think I could make myself a proper noblewoman." Ridley playfully shoved Grace. "But Glenbard is my home; you are right, there."

"It is both our homes now," Grace pointed out.

Ridley sat in a great chair Henry placed before the fireplace; turned sideways, hanging her feet over the armrest. "I'm glad Marcus finally decided to call you back."

Jack mentioned he didn't know if Marcus had apprised Ridley of the whole situation, so Grace didn't speak of it. And there was no way to ever really know what the Princess of Thieves knew or didn't, so instead of commenting how she was to be used as bait, Grace said, "He must deem it safe for my return then. Is Mac reined in?"

A strange and angry light entered her friend's face. "Hardly! The bloody snake is as slippery as ever. He ain't staying in Glenbard, that's for sure, because not a soul has seen him. Or so people claim. Marcus thinks he's moved on for now, but is sure of his return." She jumped out of the chair. "It's fair dangerous in Glenbard with the King of Thieves so on edge, and there's no tellin' where some loyalties lie. But I tell ya, Gracie, I'll be glad to have you back. I've never been shut out from Guild affairs, but Marcus and the others haven't been much in the mood for conversation these days. I need my friend back."

Ridley obviously wasn't aware of any of the background scheming. Jack seemed to know more and that was odd, seeing as how he wasn't one of Marcus's real followers. What sort of scheme was Marcus working out?

~*~*~

Henry hugged Grace goodbye and then did the same to Jack and Ridley. They stayed for two days in his company, but Grace had decided it was time for them to head home. Ridley wanted to stay longer to enjoy a noblewoman's luxuries and Henry laughed; offering his home to Grace's friends whenever they decided to return. Henry would miss the company the three provided. They were a breath of fresh air compared to his usual solitary surroundings.

"Come and visit me whenever you feel like it. The doors of my home are always open to you and your friends in Glenbard."

"I'm sure we'll be around soon enough," Jack said. He mounted Pilgrim and turned the horse toward the road. Ridley was already in the saddle on her horse, Jewel.

Grace hugged Henry one last time before mounting Olwen. "Thank you for everything, Henry. I am going to miss you." Then she turned her mare toward the road and the three set off, back toward Glenbard.

~*~*~

One more day of traveling lay before Jack, Ridley and Grace. They had set up camp on the side of the road and were finishing their dinner. Grace took the first night watch while Jack stretched out on his back to watch the moon. If they set out at sunrise, they could make it to the Angel by noon. Ridley decided a quick wash in a nearby stream was in order, and they could hear her splashing in the water.

"You really think it will come down to using me as bait?"

Jack rolled onto his stomach and propped himself up on his elbows. "I couldn't say. Not like the King makes his plans known to me." Jack read Grace's expressions by the firelight and shook his head. "I hope you're not planning on picking any fights when we get back. You're not such a skilled knife fighter or wrestler that you should go bringing big, nasty brutes out of their filthy holes."

The dagger! Grace suddenly remembered the mysterious dagger. She pulled it from her saddle bag and held it out to Jack. "Kit said it was from Escion. Is it yours?"

"It *was* mine, but now it is yours. After your incident in the woods and then the tavern brawl, I knew you needed to learn how to fight with more than a sword. That is my great-grandfather's dagger, given to the eldest son of my family for generations. Now I'm going to get some sleep. Wake me when you are too tired to keep watch."

"Wait – you really wanted me to have it? I can afford my own weaponry. This is a family heirloom."

Jack groaned and sat up completely, scooting closer to Grace. "They aren't my family anymore, and haven't been for a long time." He took the blade from Grace and inspected it by the light of the fire. "It was the first gift I have given in years," he whispered.

Grace didn't bother with words. She leaned in close and kissed Jack; surprised when he kissed her back. The moment passed as Ridley's footsteps heralded her approach.

"Stubborn *and* forward," Jack said. "Gods, what will happen to me?" he teased; smiling over at Grace.

"What jokes are you two telling? Did I miss a bawdy exchange?"

Grace felt her cheeks burning and thanked the shadows of the firelight. "Only the bawdiest joke ever told," she said.

"And you missed it," Jack continued. "Because an old man such as myself needs more sleep than young ladies such as yourselves." He tweaked Grace's nose when Ridley turned her back to unfurl her bedroll and gave her a quick kiss before returning to his sleeping spot.

~*~*~

Grace had felt unwanted when she left the port city, but many of the regulars in the tavern were pleased to see her return. Upon entering the inn, many welcomed Grace and her companions. It was warming to see that she wasn't an outcast everywhere.

Ridley hugged Grace again and said, "Grace, I am so happy you came back with us. There really is no other female around for me to talk to, except maybe the old brothel women or the surly barmaid. I love them all, but it's so nice to have someone around here close to my age. Come on, I have a surprise for you in your room. I had this all planned before leaving to retrieve you."

Ridley took Grace up to her old room in the Angel's stables. On her bed were several ornate dresses unlike anything Grace had ever seen. They were clearly meant for the summer seasons and were bright, happy colors, which many in Cesernan did not wear. In addition to the dresses, a few pairs of silk slippers were left for her as well.

"Donald returned two days before I left and brought native dresses of Nareroc back for you. He also said your birthday is barely a week away, so you can expect a surprise from Marcus and me soon. I'll be sure to get you somethin' pretty to match the dresses…earrings, maybe. I know Marcus won't see the need for a young lady such as you to own those things. He only likes to give practical gifts."

Grace threw her arms around Ridley and hugged her tightly. "You don't have to get me anything! Just the thought is the nicest thing you could do."

"Come on now, you shouldn't be surprised. We love you around here. You've been the friendliest person to come into the Angel or even Glenbard for the longest time. And you've done wonders with Jack. He used to just sit in his corner, never speak, and drink all day. He talks more and he's less surly with everyone now that you're here. He's actually pleasant to talk to. And don't think I was blind to his lingering stares," Ridley pressed her hands to her heart, "as you two fawned over each other. As if I wouldn't notice!" Grace smiled and blushed a bit, and then gave Ridley a playful push. "Don't forget there are other people who are happy you're back."

Certainly Marcus liked her as an ally. Jack liked her too, but Grace had no idea she meant so much to the other people around the tavern.

"If Marcus tries to send you away again I'll fight him tooth and nail."

"I don't think we have to worry about that for a while. Now where is Donald? I need to speak to him."

"There is still work to be done on the trade ship he was on. He won't be back until well after nightfall."

Work. Grace groaned. She had forgotten all about her own work. "I should see Mayhew today. I suppose I am out of the stable job by now. Even though Marcus spoke with him, I was gone longer than I should have been."

"Mayhew was furious those first few days after you left, but Marcus persuaded him to let you keep your job. He reminded Mayhew that you lasted longer than some of the boys who used to work for him."

"Oh dear, I should go speak to him and get right back to work then."

Grace shooed Ridley out so she could change into her work breeches and shirt. She headed into the stables and found Mayhew brushing down Pilgrim. It appeared Olwen had already been taken back to Marcus's private stables. When Mayhew saw Grace, he shot her a nasty glance.

"Look who finally decided to return." He pushed the brush into her hands. "Finish brushing down Pilgrim. Tomorrow you'll muck out all the stables, polish all the saddles and bridles, and milk Jim's dairy cow. For now, make sure every animal in this stable has plenty of clean water and food. And you're not leaving until it's all done!" Mayhew stormed out of the stable and Grace began her work.

She worked quickly and without complaint. Many of the horses seemed glad to have her gentle touch back instead of Mayhew and his rough hands and gruff voice. Grace noted, and quite gladly, that Hammer was gone, although she knew Mac and Hammer weren't gone for good.

As she worked, she hummed a little tune she picked up from some of the sailors who came through the Angel. She couldn't recall many of the words, so she just hummed it. As she drew near the end, a voice sang out the last line, "'And she said her name was Rose'," Jack's voice finished the song for her.

"I didn't fancy you to be a singer," Grace said, and put down the bucket of water she was hauling.

Jack picked it up. "Let me help you. Your presence is wanted for dinner, and no doubt you're not leaving here until Mayhew is satisfied."

"I only have to see to it that every animal is fed and watered now."

"You take care of their food and I'll get the water." They worked together in silence until only Pilgrim's food and water remained.

"Jack?"

"Hmm?" He put down the water bucket to look at her. Her gray eyes sparkled as she got onto her tiptoes to reach his mouth and gave him a soft kiss.

She hadn't kissed him since that night on the road, due to the fact that Ridley was always watching them. Her face flushed with embarrassment, but still she smiled as she moved away. Knowing the upbringing of noble ladies, this was too forward of her.

He patted the top of her head. "My little chick, you are a strange breed." He bent forward and kissed her forehead first, then returned the kiss on her lips; running his fingers through her hair, loosening her ponytail. He pulled away, but let his hand linger on her cheek.

"Jack! Don't distract the girl!" Grace jumped back at the sound of Mayhew's voice.

"We're hurrying, you cranky old man," Jack growled. He smiled at Grace and picked up the water buckets again.

~*~*~

Donald sat with Ridley and chatted over various things. He wasn't really interested in what was being said, he just wanted to see Grace again. He was filled with fear when he first learned she had run off. Now she was back and Mayhew wouldn't even let him into the stables to see her. The old man shooed Donald away from the stable entrance, yelling that she had too much work to do.

The inn was bustling with activity that night. Marcus was in his usual seat of power, dispensing the members of the Guild to go where they could to do their thieving. Ridley was bouncing back and forth, talking to Donald and helping Marcus. Only Jack wasn't in his usual spot. Donald hadn't seen him yet that evening.

Finally Grace emerged from the kitchen area, looking more than a little drawn. Jack was with her, leading her by the hand, but once they came into the common room he released her. Donald was too distracted at seeing Grace again to notice. He jumped from his seat and left Ridley in mid-sentence.

He pulled Grace into a great bear hug. "You caused so much trouble for me! When Ridley said you had been sent away, I feared the worst."

"She didn't mention Henry?"

"Well yes, but all I heard at first was, 'Grace has left the inn.'" He led her to the table he shared with Ridley and Jack sat with them. This time both Ridley and Donald took note of how closely they sat to one another.

"I am sorry, Donald." Grace reached across the table and clasped Donald's arm comfortingly. "You know I never meant to distress you. Please order our dinners," she said suddenly. "Donald, will you come with me?"

~*~*~

Donald sat at the little desk in Grace's room while Grace lay on her stomach on the bed. Jack and Ridley came and went with their food; leaving the Arganis natives alone in Grace's stable room. Since Grace's injury the two had not spent much time in each other's company.

Now she listened with great interest to the story of Donald's journey to the spice islands of Nareroc, and hoped she would one day get the chance to go there herself. But when his tale was finished, she had to start in on her own.

She told him about Mac and how she knew he was the man who stabbed her in the woods, and then she told him about Marcus's cousin and how she was the woman Mac killed in front of Grace that night. Finally, she told him of the scuffle between her and Mac and Jack in the stables. She even confessed that Marcus had guessed her secret. Just how, neither one could fathom. As her tale grew to a close, the suspicions and theories began.

"And why do you think Mac kidnapped her in the first place? What would killing Marcus's cousin have to do with taking his throne?"

"I don't have the slightest idea. Marcus doesn't trust him, but he pretends to believe Mac's tale of finding his cousin on the side of the road beside her 'murderer', who was killed by The Death Dealer. Mac is brewing trouble. Marcus knows it, but hasn't been able to call him out of hiding. I hope that with my return, I can find him."

"Good luck. No one has heard a word of Mac for three days, I've been told. Rumors at the dock were that Marcus drove him out. Other rumors say he fled Cesernan altogether."

"Can you keep your eyes and ears open down by the docks? I can get most any news I need here, but I cannot be all over Glenbard at once."

"I can see what people know, at least. There are a few members of the Guild who worked on board with me," Donald said. "Just try not to get too far in. Mac has beaten you twice and I'm sure he could do it again. Marcus cannot protect you if you go out looking for trouble."

"I will be fine. I just have to keep Marcus and the Guild blind and deaf to what I'm doing until I know something for sure. You and Jack can help with that part." Grace rolled off her bed and pulled her Death Dealer jerkin from her trunk.

Someone knocked on the door, causing Donald to jump slightly. Grace returned the jerkin to its spot and closed the trunk. "Hello?"

"It's Marcus."

Donald rose. "I'll leave you to talk with him in private. No need for me to hear any of this. But please be careful." He touched Grace's shoulder and kissed her cheek.

Opening the door, he bowed his head to Marcus and left. The King of Thieves entered and closed the door. "Welcome home. I would have liked to welcome you properly, but my dear, we have business to attend to." He sat in the chair Donald had so recently occupied.

He looked old these days. The rumors flying around Glenbard said that for almost a decade, no one had challenged Marcus for his throne in earnest. Many tried, but if what Ridley and others said rang true, no one had ever gone to the lengths

Mac was going to now. Grace hated to think it, but it was very possible that the fierce old man could lose his seat of power to scum like Mac.

"My leaving didn't draw Mac out, but I expect you think my return will?"

"Nah – originally I believed his pride was hurt because he couldn't conquer you, but now I think he has learned to have as much patience as he needs. Mac figures he'll have his chance at you when he sits on my throne. I've called you back because only one person has the ability to sneak around this city and the surrounding woods."

Grace removed her jerkin and hood from the sack under her bed. "I can try to track down Mac tonight."

~*~*~

At one o'clock that morning, Grace went out into the dark alone. Since first coming to Glenbard, she had discovered a weak line in the gate that circled the city for protection. Using any of the roads to head out into the wooded areas was impossible, but Grace had found a small hole she used to crawl through that led directly out of the city. Crawling through the muck and mud, Grace emerged on the other side of the city walls.

The last anyone heard in regards to Mac was that he was moving about close to Glenbard. These, of course, were marketplace rumors and based on the sightings reported by traveling merchants, who had a tendency to exaggerate the truth. Still, Marcus advised Grace to take heed of the reported sightings. If their eyes had not deceived them, Mac and his band were some five miles east of the city.

Trying not to crunch the leaves too much underneath her feet, Grace moved about as best as she could in the dark until a dim fire came into view. Grace kept low to the ground and moved forward. Voices murmured, but she wasn't able to make out anything distinct. She needed to get closer. Grace grabbed a low branch of a nearby tree and climbed to a higher branch before crawling out as far as she could. She had a better view from her new spot and she could better hear those down by the fire. This move was risky because if just one person looked up into the trees, they might see her eyes peering from her hood. For the moment no one looked, and she easily blended into the shadows.

There were about twenty men sitting around the fire. Grace recognized several of them to be lesser members of the Guild, and then she spotted Mac. He stood beside the fire and began to address the men that sat around him. "Everything is in place, then. More of my men will be arriving from Salatia any day now, and then all we have to do is lure Marcus away from Thom and those other grovelin' fools in the Guild. We will dethrone the King of Thieves and I will take his place. Then you rogues will have your day. Marcus don't believe in takin' women as part of our plunder or in killin' those that get in the way. Once he, Thom and Ridley are taken care of, there's no one to stand in our way."

"How do you plan on gettin' Marcus out here, anyway?" Grace recognized the voice of Geary; a relatively well-known member of the Guild. Grace had never pegged him as a dishonorable fiend like Mac.

"Leave that to me," Mac growled. "It shouldn't take much to lure Marcus out. He just needs the right incentive."

Grace crawled back toward the trunk of the tree. There was no time to waste. She scrambled down the tree and hurried back toward the city as quietly as a mouse. Crawling back through the gate's hole, she took to running again; keeping to the shadows and the alleys. Marcus lived on the fringe of Glenbard's lower city, so getting there unseen was easy. The city seemed almost designed that way so thieves could move about easier.

The lights in the narrow two story house were all extinguished. Waiting until morning wouldn't have hurt, but Marcus needed to know now since Grace didn't hang around long enough to hear the rest of Mac's plot. Knowing he would strike soon was all she needed. Unsheathing her sword, she pounded on the door with the hilt. A few minutes passed before candlelight appeared in the kitchen window. A drowsy Thom opened the door. Upon seeing the executioner's hood outlined in his candle's light, he dropped it; extinguishing the flame.

"You! What business brings you here so late?"

Grace pushed past Thom. "I need to speak to Marcus and it cannot wait until morning! Please wake him for me."

Thom was tired and groggy. He was a loyal servant and friend to the King of Thieves, and knew urgency when he heard it, even if it was only in troubled whispers. "Wait here."

Overhead, Grace heard Marcus order Ridley and Thom back to bed. Marcus came down the stairs in only a pair of tattered old breeches. "Well?"

"I am truly sorry to disturb you, but it's about Mac. I saw his camp tonight. He has at least twenty men with him, and he said more were to arrive soon from Salatia."

"Pox and rot!" Marcus pounded his right fist into his left hand. "Salatia has had problems for two seasons now. I should have known Mac was inciting them. His brother lives there, and for the past year he has spent much of his time there."

"What do you plan to do? Geary is among Mac's number."

"That is no surprise. He has tried in the past for my throne, but was too weak to take it. He would ally himself with Mac despite all my efforts to keep him close." Marcus smiled and patted Grace's shoulder. "I will have a plan to handle the situation. Right now I won't raise the alarm. If we start a war in the city, Frederick's men will be on us and no one will be left to defend my people. Go home and get some sleep. I will call for your aid if it is needed."

Marcus climbed the stairs back to his room and Grace left the house thinking about the fate that lay before her friend.

"Why exactly did you need to see the King so late?" Grace looked up and saw Jack standing beside Marcus's fence.

"What are you doing here?"

"Walking home from the Angel. I do leave, you know."

Grace sighed in relief. She was afraid he'd been following her around. "It was about Mac. I was out tonight and overheard his plan to dethrone Marcus. I had to warn him." Grace stood beside Jack and saw the doubt written all over his face.

Jack took Grace firmly by the shoulders and steered her up

the street. "And?"

"Marcus told me to wait and that he would call for help if he needed it."

"Marcus *is* going to need it. Rumors at the Angel after everyone turned in revolved around Mac and the sightings people have had of him hiding out in the woods. There could be a war here for the common born, and if you meddle further into these affairs, you'll be the spark that ignites it. You know better than most that playing with fire is dangerous."

Jack was afraid that she was getting involved too heavily with the Guild, and that was a dangerous game. Others had tried to dethrone the King of Thieves before. The king who sat before Marcus had usurped the throne from his own mother, and then he met a nasty end by the hand of Marcus when he was too ineffectual for the thieving game. And though Jack had only known of the Thieves' Guild for seven years, he saw many men try to usurp the throne from Marcus in that time. Many ventures to do so ended in bloody confrontations for the men, as well as those who followed them.

He knew Grace had no idea what she was getting herself into. If Mac was successful they would find out that Grace tried to help Marcus, and who knows what would happen to her after that?

Jack took her by the arm and walked her back toward the Angel. "I hope you're not planning on doing anything rash concerning Mac. He'll kill you the next time you fight, that I can say with confidence."

"I'm not going to just sit back and let him hurt my friends."

"Neither are your friends. Leave this to Marcus and Thom. You just go back to fighting petty rogues in the wild and let Marcus do what he does. You'll be safer that way."

"Do you even care about Marcus? I could help protect him!"

"I care more about someone protecting *you*."

"Why? Marcus is just as much your friend as he is mine."

"Marcus is a grown man. You, Death Dealer, are a small, hooded, and stubborn person who will get hurt if rashness prevails." Jack stopped them in the alley behind the Angel.

"Don't be stupid. Do what Marcus said. Sit back and wait." He bent forward, pulled her hood up and kissed her softly.

Jack pulled back and stroked her cheek. Turning on his heel, he disappeared into the shadows.

Thirteen

Grace had been back in Glenbard for three days. Her birthday was two days away, but she wasn't able to muster any excitement for it. Geary tried to lure Marcus from his home early one morning, but Marcus turned him away with many harsh words. Grace was unsure exactly what was said, but she was tremendously worried that Jack was right and war would erupt.

No one had heard from Mac since the day Kay left the city, and an uneasy feeling fell on Grace. Donald told her there was little to fear, but what did he know? In a few days he would be headed back toward the Nareroc Islands, unaware of what was really happening in Glenbard.

On the third night after Marcus and The Death Dealer met to discuss Mac, Grace was having a troubled sleep. She chased something, yet she could never catch it. Stopping her hunt, she lay in a grassy field and watched the clouds that threatened to rain upon her. Suddenly a weight pressed on her chest, and fighting to wake up, Grace opened her eyes to find a black wolf standing on her chest. Its eyes gleamed silver with no pupils.

Get up! a voice broke through Grace's thoughts; terrifying her. The voice echoed through her entire mind; howling through it like wind howled through a tunnel. This animal was blessed by the gods and chose to come into Grace's life. The wolf jumped down and looked at her pointedly. *Get thee gone, Death Dealer! The villain has made his move!*

Grace needed no more urging. She was dressed and out her window in record time.

~*~*~

Port side, Jack awoke to the same howling voice. It simply said *"Thom"* to him. Needing no more urging, Jack dressed and headed to Marcus's. The door to his house was open, nearly broken off its hinges. Inside, dishes were broken, the table was overturned, the chairs were smashed, and poor Thom was bound, gagged and unconscious.

Running out to the well near Marcus's, Jack retrieved a

bucket of water. Instead of dousing Thom, he untied the poor fellow and found a ladle to pour some water onto his face. He only groaned at first, but when Jack dumped the rest of the bucket on his head, Thom sat straight up. His breath was ragged and his eyes were full of concern and anger.

He took hold of Jack's shoulders and pinched him hard. "They've taken Marcus and Ridley! I came home from running messages and found two of Mac's men looting the house. They spared me...I don't know why, but they did."

"Be thankful they have." Jack ripped up a tablecloth to bandage Thom's wrist, which had been cut by a dull knife and irritated by the rope used to bind him.

"I have to raise the alarm!" Thom tried to get to his feet but Jack forced him down.

"Think sense! You're in no condition to move yourself. Stay here and I will go to the Angel and raise an alarm."

"But—"

"Stay, let me get you a healer. Don't risk your life just yet."

Jack helped Thom into what was left of his bed before heading off again. Outside Marcus's house, the silver-eyed wolf sat. *Don't raise the alarm just yet. I have sent the Thief King aid.*

"You can't mean Grace," he snarled.

Mac is waiting for a large scale attack from Marcus's followers. That is why Thom lives. At dawn you may raise the alarm, but tonight his men are poised and ready for attack.

"And what of Grace? They won't be prepared for The Death Dealer to appear?"

Mac believes she will lead the offensive. Alone, she can sneak into the camp and free the captives, but only if she is given the chance. Wait an hour or more before calling Marcus's followers forth. By then Grace will have freed her friends, or died trying. If the alarm is sounded now, everyone will know who The Death Dealer is. That is as much a danger to her as to Mac.

Jack growled and jumped at the wolf, but it took off into the dark. He stalked off to the temple district to make hasty prayers to Kamaria, Ciro, and Diggery for the safe delivery of Marcus and

Ridley, and most especially for Grace.

~*~*~

Grace pushed herself to the spot she had been only a few precious nights before. If it wasn't for the executioner's hood, Grace's face would have been severely cut by the whipping branches. Unlike the last time she spied on Mac, she wasn't being careful or quiet. She ignored the stinging sensation she felt underneath her hood and stopped running for a moment.

There had been a fire in this spot recently, and she guessed Mac and his group put it out in the last few hours. These men were no fools; they covered their tracks well. Grace guessed they went north, but their tracks led off in all directions. Mac must have guessed their secret hideaway was not so secret, after all. After Marcus sent Geary away, Mac probably guessed he was being watched closer than he believed.

Enraged by it all, Grace kicked a charred log across the campsite. Mac was already one step ahead, and if she took the wrong path it would cost her precious hours. Already she was wasting time trying to guess which way the real path was. She took off north. The next largest city was north of Glenbard and she figured Mac might try heading out there. It would take days of travel to get there, but if Mac had enough of a head start and had horses with him, Grace knew she would never catch him.

Something growled and barked. Grace turned in her tracks and saw the large black wolf again. It barked angrily at Grace, although it made no move toward her, so she slowly walked toward the northern path. Seeing this, the wolf leapt after her and blocked the path.

It was steering her away from the northern route. Then Grace noticed something odd...the wolf's silver eyes sparkled in the dark. Tales had been told and many legends consisted of a wolf just like this, and Grace, now fully awake, understood what was happening.

"If you really are Diggery, guardian of the lost, then show me the right path."

The wolf seemed pleased that Grace finally understood. She

bounded past the girl and headed with all speed down a western path. Grace wasted no time. Her legs ached from running so much already, but she pushed forward. She lost sight of the wolf as its black fur concealed it in the darkness, but Grace could still hear the swift movement of her great padded feet.

The large black wolf set a grueling pace and Grace felt her muscles begin to tire. She wanted to help her friends, but now faced with the actual task, she wondered if she could do it. She needed help, but she fled Glenbard without calling for aid from the thieves. What kind of foolishness was that?

She stopped and strained her hearing. The wolf could no longer be heard ahead. "I failed. I failed everyone...Marcus, Ridley, myself." She sank to her knees and pounded the ground with her fists. Hot tears of frustration poured down her face, soaking the hood. "I...need a...help..." she cried out to no one in particular.

The wolf came to her side and licked the hood. Grace removed it and the animal gently cleaned the tears from her face. Diggery threw back her head and let out a howl that shook the entire wood. Grace suddenly felt filled with a new strength. She rose to her feet again and continued on.

~*~*~

Grace walked well into the night, always keeping the wolf in her view. Suddenly the wolf stopped and Grace stopped beside her. The wolf began to walk slowly ahead, crouching low to the ground.

A fire came into Grace's view. It was small and dim from where she stood, but she guessed that the wolf had brought her to Mac's hideout.

"I suppose I'm on my own from here?"

The wolf growled a little and snuffed at Grace's hand. *You will not be alone, I promise.* Grace was a bit shocked. She couldn't see the wolf completely in the dark, but she swore she saw it smile. Returning the hood to her head, Grace patted the wolf softly, wondering if she was out of line petting Diggery.

Grace snuck forward slowly. There was no telling how many

guards Mac had posted about. The black of her clothes would help conceal her, but once she was closer to that fire, her shadow would give her away. The thought she might die that night kept running through Grace's head.

She knew she wasn't ready to fight Mac, and this time Jack wouldn't be there to come to her rescue. "You don't need someone to rescue you," Grace whispered to herself.

Grace had a clear view of the camp and saw a large tent on the outskirts. Mac suddenly came out with a flagon of wine. "The King is almost ready to abdicate to me!" Mac shouted, and his men threw out raucous cheers.

Grace now knew where Marcus was, but how would she get inside? It was possible to sneak around and cut through the back of the tent, but not without making a lot of noise. Even in a drunken state the men would hear her cutting the fabric of the tent. Waiting for them all to fall asleep was no good either. Mac was probably waiting for Marcus to give in, and then he would kill him in a show of strength.

Luck was on Grace's side, though. The great wolf, Diggery, darted past Grace and jumped into the circle of Mac's men. It snapped angrily and began attacking whoever was near. When it howled, the horses of the camp went completely mad. The mutiny of the animals caused enough noise and enough of a distraction for Grace to sneak around to the back of the tent.

She used Jack's dagger and cut a door for herself in the fabric. Grace slipped in and saw Marcus and Ridley lying on the ground, bloodied and beaten, tied to one another. Ridley was in terrible shape, but Marcus seemed to have his wits about him.

"Death Dealer? You've come to help us?"

Grace nodded.

"Death...Dealer?" Ridley moaned and tried to open her eyes. Grace was filled with rage as she truly saw what had happened. Ridley had been beaten so badly her eyes were swollen shut and her nose was broken. This was probably how Mac convinced Marcus to abdicate. There was no telling what else he'd done to the girl, and she didn't want to know.

175

Grace cut them free and helped Marcus to his feet. In turn, he lifted Ridley up over his shoulder. "Run east. Hide among the shadows. I'll distract them here."

"Thank you, Death Dealer." Marcus disappeared through Grace's little door. Soon he was gone into the night.

That was as far as Grace had thought out her plan. She hadn't given much thought to how she would escape. The wolf howled again and Grace heard a large number of running feet. "After the demon! It's going into the forest!" someone yelled.

"Let me get my good sword!" Mac's voice. He was coming back into the tent.

Grace drew her sword and prepared herself. Mac threw open the tent flap and stopped dead in his tracks.

"You again? I see my last gift wasn't enough to keep you away." Mac picked up his sword. "I enjoyed marking you once. I'm gonna love doing it again."

When he lunged Grace sidestepped, and Mac ripped another hole into the tent. The space was too small, but Grace couldn't risk being in the open. The rogues in Mac's group would tear her limb from limb. She had a slim chance of survival within the tent, so at least there was a little bit of hope. Mac lifted his sword into a high arc and brought it crashing down against Grace's. Grace believed in honor in fighting, but she also had the wits to see there would be no honor in this fight, and there was a chance it would end like their first fight had. So she used a little trick Ridley taught her. She waited until Mac went for a lower hit and then she kicked at the wrist on his sword arm. He dropped the sword and with a second well placed kick, Grace caught him squarely in the chest.

He staggered back from her, but his recovery time was amazingly swift. Grace grabbed his sword, but Mac had plenty of other weapons in his tent. He picked up a huge ax and swung at Grace's head. She ducked in time to feel the swing of the ax move the air around her head.

"You're fast, boy, I'll give ya that. But did you really think you'd best 'ole Mac? You're just a little boy playing big boy games." Grace dodged another swing of the ax, but this time she smashed Mac's right hand with the hilt of his sword. Something cracked and he loosened his grip with that hand.

"I am not a boy!" Grace quickly exposed her face so Mac would see who fought him. Just as quickly, she pulled the hood down again.

"*You?* This is gonna be more fun than I thought." Mac dropped the ax. "I'm goin' to give you the beating you deserve, and then I'll show you how to respect a man."

Mac jumped at her and brought her crashing to the ground, and her sword flew from her hand. He got off one good solid punch to her chest, but not another. Grace used her knees and made contact with his stomach. When he tightened his midsection, she used her foot to throw him off. As she scrambled to her feet, Mac grabbed her by the ankle and she came crashing back down.

Mac had a solid hold on her left foot, but he neglected her right one. Grace used this to her advantage and kicked him hard in the face. This time she was able to get to her feet, and Mac staggered up as well. Despite his injuries he was lightning fast, and Grace was only able to land one punch before he lifted her over his head.

The next thing Grace knew she was sailing through her newly made door and hitting the ground with a great deal of force. She couldn't be sure, but she thought she landed on a large, sharp rock. She didn't think she was bleeding, but the pain was excruciating. It snaked up her side, adding to the ache she already carried in her muscles.

She got to her feet and looked about for a new weapon. When Mac appeared in the hole she just flew out of, she realized he was holding the ax again.

"I've had enough of these games." Mac let out a primal scream and ran for Grace; bringing the ax high for the final death blow.

But he didn't expect the final trick Grace had waiting. She pulled the Escion dagger out of her belt, and when Mac was close enough she thrust it forward. The ax clattered to the ground and Mac gasped like a fish out of water as the knife lodged in his chest. Grace felt his blood on her hand as she gave the dagger a savage turn. He fell to the ground and joined his ax.

"Hey! Behind here!" someone called. Grace ignored her pain and took off running through the woods. "Hey, wait a minute!"

~*~*~

Grace was so tired, but she kept running. Although her body was slowing down, she still thought she was outrunning them. If she just kept moving they'd never catch her. Mac's men would never get her. But then they did.

Hurt and confused from her fight with Mac, Grace failed to understand how close behind her follower was until he had a good strong hold on her from behind.

"Let me go!" She screamed and used her elbows and what was left of her strength to try and fight him off. "Let...me...*go!*"

"Grace, stop fighting me!" Jack's voice stopped Grace dead in her fight. He was the one chasing after her, calling for her to stop.

She sank to her knees and panted; looking straight forward into the darkness.

"Grace, are you all right? Are you hurt?"

"No. Well yes, but no. He's dead...and his men...I thought they were chasing me."

Jack removed her hood and smoothed Grace's hair. "No, the Guild arrived sometime while you and Mac were fighting in the tent. I raised the alarm, as Diggery instructed." She looked at him, shocked. He held her chin. "The wolf saw to it that you weren't alone."

The confusion began to clear in Grace's head. The adrenaline rush was wearing off and Grace's body was calming down. "Marcus? Marcus and Ridley?"

"Both fine. We found them staggering back to the city. And Thom is going to be fine as well. Everyone has you to thank, though I suppose no one will know it."

Jack looked at Grace's hands, coated in blood. He pulled out his water skin and poured a little over her hands.

"I beat him, Jack," she said while Jack rubbed what he could of the blood from her hands. "I didn't think I could, but I did. It was horrible to see him die like that, caught so unawares by the dagger. I watched his life drain away." She began to cry; heaving in deep breaths until they turned into hiccups.

"Don't think about it now."

Grace met Jack's eyes in the darkness. They glinted a little in the moonlight and she sighed heavily. Jack pulled her into a hug and planted a soft kiss on her lips.

"I killed him," she said again. "What have I done?"

"We have to get you back to Glenbard," he said, and helped Grace to her feet. "Wait here and I'll get Pilgrim." He put her executioner's hood in her hands. "Put this on."

Fourteen

The day Grace rescued Marcus and Ridley was a blur. She returned to the Angel just before she needed to report to Mayhew. Her wounds weren't severe, so she covered the bruises and worked as though nothing happened. She was excused from duty at the midday meal because Marcus wanted a word privately. Everyone believed the King of Thieves wanted to tell her she didn't need to fear Mac anymore.

He was tired, beaten and bruised. "You look well, Grace. If you're worried, people think Thom is The Death Dealer."

"How is Ridley?"

"We took her to a healer. She'll live. Her nose will be crooked and she may have a few scars, but it could have been worse. You can see her tomorrow; she'll be sleeping right now."

Marcus pulled out a chair for Grace. He sat on the table in front of her and smiled down at her slightly. "How are you? No noticeable bruises, at least. Jack told me he brought you home, though you insisted on climbing through the mud to get back into the city." She giggled for the first time all day. "Mac's dead."

Grace sobered up completely. "I see his death face every time I blink. Don't tell Jack, but I vomited as soon as I came back to the Angel. I killed a man early this season…it was an accident. But I *murdered* Mac. I wanted to forget the first man I killed, the one I didn't even know by name, but now I never can."

Marcus took her hand in his. The touch was warm and fatherly. "You can't forget, although I wish you could. I remember all of the lives I've taken. The memories are rarer and rarer, but some days, well, I see their faces clear as day. Usually on the brink of wakefulness or in the late watches, but they're there."

"I am turning into a coldblooded murderer."

"No!" The word sucked all the air out and replaced it with tension. "You are a good person; I have seen it. And I will not let you fall from this virtuous path you've placed yourself on." He smoothed out her hair; her ponytail streaming out through his fingers. "Back to work with you. I can't keep you from Mayhew all day."

~*~*~

That night, Grace found a gift of a new jerkin on her bed. Marcus left a note saying it was an early birthday gift, and that if it didn't fit, he would have one made that did.

Though the gift warmed her heart, she couldn't bring herself to look at The Death Dealer hood. She'd killed two men now and the guilt weighed heavily on her mind. By her hand, two men had gone from this world to the next. She ran her fingers over the leather, enjoying the smooth touch, but this was a cruel reminder of what she had done. After a good, long cry she went immediately to see Ridley, though her body cried for sleep.

When she arrived at the temple to visit, the priestess looked angry. In a vow of silence, the priestess wrote that Marcus knew there should be no visitors.

"I am a cousin. Certainly family can come by?" Grace said after reading the note. A scowl was her only response, but the priestess led the way.

Poor Ridley was propped up on her pillows. Her face was a dark green and purple mess. A healer tried to set her nose, but a lump still protruded.

"You came!" she rasped. Grace grabbed her hands. "Marcus said no visitors, but you came."

"I had to put a few coins into the alms box and promise some cleaning around here, but I had to see you. Tell me everything."

"They came so suddenly. Geary was leading them. They knocked me out but I came to in that filthy tent." Tears welled up in her eyes. Grace hugged her as gently as she could and let her own tears coat her friend's hair. "I don't remember everything," Ridley continued after a few minutes of silent sobbing between them. "But I think it's better that I don't. He might have gone so far as to kill me just to get at Marcus's throne. Then The Death Dealer came, and I felt it was all a dream. I couldn't see well, but he was there. I heard Marcus say his name. He rescued us! Then I woke up here. He's dead, isn't he?"

Grace took a breath and nodded. "Marcus had a private word with me. He wanted me to know I was safe from Mac."

"We are all safe, and all because of that valiant hero."

Grace sat up and talked with Ridley. She tried to keep conversation light, because each time Mac was brought up, both girls teared up. After an hour and much prodding, Grace confided in Ridley what was happening between her and Jack. Even in her sick bed, the girl managed an ecstatic whoop. That was when Grace was removed from the sick room for being too disruptive.

~*~*~

Grace looked into the eyes of the Diggery statue. It wasn't the same as looking into the eyes of the deity in wolf form. She sighed and hung her head.

"It is my fault a man died." Grace heard the door to the temple open and she didn't need to turn to know Jack was sauntering up to her.

"It is because of you that your friends still live," Jack said simply. He wrapped an arm around her shoulder and kissed her temple.

Grace tried to pull away but he held fast to her. "I don't know if I can ever wear my hood again. I dreamed I was afloat on a river of blood last night. If I go out again to right 'wrongs', the sea will swallow me."

The temple was empty. No one wanted to pray when there was money to be made or fun to be had. Jack sat in a pew and pulled Grace onto his lap. "Ridley was walloped. She couldn't even see when they took her to the healer. She will be bruised for days, her nose will be tender for weeks, and she will carry those scars for life. But – and my little chick, this is key – she will live. So will Marcus. You saved two people. That is how you should view this."

"How can I live with the guilt of causing his death?"

"By hugging Ridley, your friend, and remembering that you almost lost her." He set her on the ground again and got to his feet. "Everyone is gathering to celebrate your birthday. Forget what happened for the evening."

Grace smiled at him, even though she had to force it.

"The cook at the Angel spent all day at Jim's request making you Shepherd's pie with potato soup and an apple cake, and you aren't even there to celebrate your own birthday."

"I felt I needed to come here first. I have been trying to think of something to offer so Diggery knows how thankful I am for her help. And to pray for forgiveness."

"She knows, and the gods look kindly on those who save lives. Now come on. The healers have allowed Ridley to come home. Everyone's waiting and Ridley is eyeing your birthday food with a ravenous look. It could all be gone by the time we get there. Now that she is on the mend, she's eating everything in sight. It's rather disgraceful."

Grace laughed and took Jack by the hand. "Then lead me to the feast. I would hate to have my birthday ruined because of a hungry little thief."

Jack put an arm around her shoulder and began leading her out, but as they reached the door he stopped. "Before I forget, it seems Henry has been quite a busy man since I met him on the road. Did you know he sent a messenger to my mother?" Grace shook her head. "Well he did, and here's the end result." Jack produced a silver chain with a winged star pendant dangling on the end.

"The symbol of Diggery?"

"My mother is a firm believer in Diggery and her protection. She felt I needed this since I am a 'lost soul.' But I say you need it more. I have never met anyone who managed to get into more trouble than you do." Jack took the liberty of putting the necklace around Grace's neck and clasping it for her.

Grace kissed his cheek and laughed. "Let's go get some apple cake."

"If there's any left to have."

Grace laughed again and let him kiss her. His fingers laced with hers. Taking Jack's advice and forgetting the unpleasantness for the evening, Grace found she was truly happy for the first time in months.

About the author:

Raised in the suburbs of Chicago, Katie Roman has been many things. Student, band geek, dog sitter, history major and consummate tea drinker, but above all things she's been a writer.

Her debut novel, Fallen Grace, was originally released Fall 2013 through Whiskey Creek Press. Visit her at www.katieromanbooks.com.

Acknowledgments

Grace has come a long way since the summer of 2006, when she was first conceived. Her story began as a way for me to survive the summer when I couldn't find a job and had little else to do until school started again. I always assumed Grace's story would end up like all my other stories: written for fun and put aside when finished. Somehow Grace's story persevered, and over the next four years I wrote two sequels when my class work allowed. The sequels have since been trashed in favor of a different direction for Grace, but *Fallen Grace* has more or less stayed the same.

The 2006 draft was put on a forum site (which is probably long since defunct now) and it was well received. The members on that site provided plenty of feedback to help Grace along her journey. Katie Bailey has also been a source of help and inspiration in writing and continuing Grace's story. She is one of the first people to have read *Fallen Grace* and she is always among the first to read and comment on my manuscripts, providing feedback and encouragement in equal measure. I never would have published this without the help and support of my mom, who went through with a red pen to fix my typos and inconsistencies and told me to writing even when I didn't want to.

Thank you to Stacy Sanford, who took the time to help me edit this for the re-release. Her work on this has been invaluable and I am eternally grateful. And to Skylar Faith, whose cover art continues to take my breath away.

It's been a long road for Grace and the people of Cesernan, and they still have more adventures to look forward to.

Also by Katie Roman

Mere Mortal

38504510R00108

Made in the USA
Charleston, SC
07 February 2015